Books by Kathryn Lasky

The Secret of Glendunny: The Haunting

The Secret of Glendunny 2: The Searchers

Faceless

Tangled in Time: The Portal

Tangled in Time 2: The Burning Queen

Guardians of Ga'Hoole Series

Wolves of the Beyond Series

Bears of the Ice Series

Horses of the Dawn Series

Daughters of the Sea Series

Glass

A Cinderella Tale

Glass

A
Cinderella
Tale

Kathryn Lasky

HARPER
An Imprint of HarperCollins*Publishers*

Library of Congress Control Number: 2023944809
ISBN 978-0-06-329402-8

Typography by Molly Fehr
24 25 26 27 28 LBC 5 4 3 2 1
First Edition

Contents

Part Four: The Silk

Part Five: The Making of a Witch

Part One

INNOCENCE

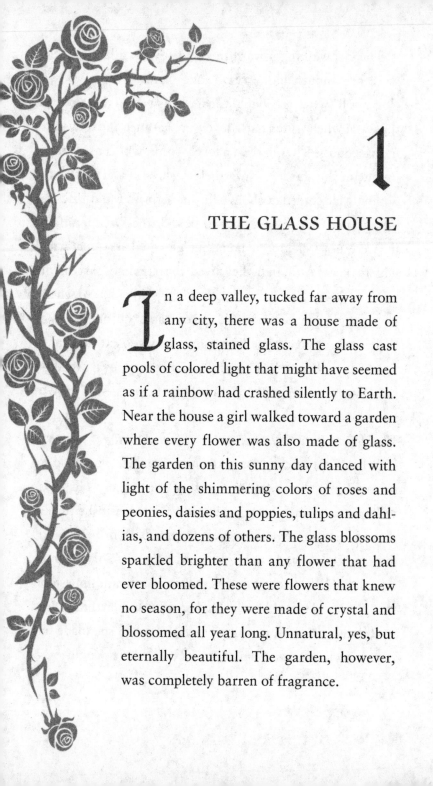

1

THE GLASS HOUSE

In a deep valley, tucked far away from any city, there was a house made of glass, stained glass. The glass cast pools of colored light that might have seemed as if a rainbow had crashed silently to Earth. Near the house a girl walked toward a garden where every flower was also made of glass. The garden on this sunny day danced with light of the shimmering colors of roses and peonies, daisies and poppies, tulips and dahlias, and dozens of others. The glass blossoms sparkled brighter than any flower that had ever bloomed. These were flowers that knew no season, for they were made of crystal and blossomed all year long. Unnatural, yes, but eternally beautiful. The garden, however, was completely barren of fragrance.

The girl walking toward the garden was called Bess. She wore her auburn hair in two long plaits, with strands of clover bells woven through. Clover bells were a delicate vine that even when wilted had a lovely appearance and only grew in this county. They carried a lovely scent, which made them unique in this garden. Nevertheless, she still sniffed the air, hoping that someday she would be surprised and discover a fragrance. But this was not to be. For the Wickham family were not perfume makers but glassmakers—renowned glassmakers. Although they lived in a remote part of the land, their renown was such that every duke and duchess, prince and princess, king and queen had exquisite pieces of their work, from chandeliers to glass bowls to extraordinary figurines of flowers and animals. For every royal wedding there was a bridal bouquet made from flowers—not grown, but blown in their furnaces. And thus was their slogan, *Wickham's Fine Crystal—not grown but blown.*

When Bess reached her sixteenth birthday, she would be initiated into the mysterious craft of turning crystals, *cristallos*, into beautiful shapes. For it was not until she turned sixteen that she would receive her *daich* from her grandmother. *Daich* was a very old word for a sack or pouch of cristallos, the fine crystals of sand, soda ash, and limestone from which glass was made. On her sixteenth birthday, Bess would also be given her blowpipe. And when she made her first object, always a small round cup, there would be a celebration. But now she stopped still in the garden of glass. As she longed for fragrance, she whispered to herself . . . "Why? Why must I be a glassmaker just because I was born into this family? Why can't I be a . . . a . . . gardener for real flowers, which smell lovely, and don't break or shatter, but simply wilt, to bloom again in another season?"

She heard footsteps behind her, running. She turned. It was her sister Olivia. Olivia's pale face was now flushed. "Has something terrible happened? What? Someone's burned in the hot shop? An explosion?"

"No, no." Olivia paused and seemed to arrange her face before speaking. She swallowed and waited several seconds. "I am so sorry to tell you this."

Why was Olivia being so formal? "Tell me what?" asked Bess. Olivia had the strangest look in her eye.

"I am sorry, Bess, but . . . it's bad news, especially for you." She slid her eyes away. *Olivia's hiding something*, Bess thought. *She doesn't want me to see it in her eyes.* "Olivia, just tell me. Did something happen to Mamma? Papa?" She glanced back at the glass house. Bess followed her eyes. The four chimneys emitted no smoke.

"No, it's Grannie . . ."

"Grannie? What?" She looked at the chimneys again. Had the ovens been shut down? There was no smoke issuing into the sky.

"She . . . she died in her sleep."

Bess caught her breath. This could not be. Her beloved grannie was dead. But that explained the smokeless chimneys. Such was the custom, an ancient one, that when a member of a glassblower's family died, the ovens were shut down for a period of mourning.

Bess studied her sister's face. There was something very odd about her expression, but Olivia's eyes wouldn't meet hers. Although the sky had suddenly turned cloudy, Olivia still wore the dark round spectacles that hung from a ribbon around her neck. The Wickhams wore these on sunny days when reflections from the glass were too powerful for their pale eyes, though the reflections had never bothered Bess.

"Too bad, Bess." Olivia sighed and tucked her lips into a flat seam, as if to conceal a smirk that threatened to escape.

"Of course it's too bad, Olivia." Tears gathered in the corner of her eyes. "It's awful!" she gasped.

"Oh, I mean too bad for you. You won't get your daich."

"What?"

"Daich of cristallos, like Grannie gave us on our sixteenth birthdays." Then she sighed. "If she had only lived another two years."

Bess's voice cracked. "Olivia, you think I'm worried about that? Not getting my cristallos because Grannie died? That is the last thing on my mind." Bess broke into a run, dodging the many sharp petals and vines of the glass flowers—the un-pickable flowers.

Followed slowly by Olivia, Bess entered their grandmother's bedroom. Everyone except Bess was wearing the dark round spectacles, for the sun's rays were splintering fiercely through the glass house. Lavinia Wickham turned toward her three daughters. "Now, dear children, it is time for the last kiss for your beloved grannie."

The three girls stepped up to the body of their grandmother in order of birth. First was Rose, who adjusted her glasses and bent over and brushed her lips to her grandmother's forehead. "Cold," she whispered to her sister Olivia. Olivia was next to step up. She bent over her grannie's head to kiss her but said nothing. Bess noticed she did not even let her lips touch the old woman's forehead.

"Oh dear," her mother said as Bess was about to step forward. "I forgot to close the body's eyes." *The body?* How had Grannie suddenly become just "the body"? Bess wondered. How had Grannie become this nameless being? The anonymity was insulting. "Will you do it, Bess, dear? Close the eyes." Bess nodded.

Her grannie had green eyes. When Bess bent over, the eyes seemed to look straight into hers. It was as if she could read them, the thoughts in Grannie's head. How could this be? But the words were clear. *Your time will come.*

"Hurry up," she heard Olivia mutter.

Bess closed the paper-thin eyelids over the sea-green eyes.

When her lips grazed her grandmother's forehead it felt warm, and not cold at all. Her father's hand gripped her shoulder. "Come along, Bess. It doesn't pay to linger over the dead."

The dead? It felt like a slap in her face. How had their grannie become simply "the dead"?

2

THAT BESS!

Bess had not been in bed long that evening when she heard a soft knock on her door.

"It's Mamma, dear."

"Come in, Mamma." She was holding something in her hands, but Bess couldn't see what it was. The moon was full and so glaring that it cast a brilliant green shadow that sliced diagonally across her mother's face. The other half of her face was a brilliant orange. "My goodness, that moon falls brightly through the stained glass. I think I need my specs." She raised the spectacles that dangled from a ribbon around her neck.

How very odd she looks, Bess thought, *with the diamond-shaped patches of color scattered on her face and dress*. All she needed was a hat with bells and she would have looked like a court jester. And then there were the two round discs of her spectacles, shading her eyes from the dizzying array of colors that fell through the colored panes of glass.

"I don't know how you do it without spectacles, dear."

"I don't always want to see the world through tinted glass. I love the light too much."

"You are a strange one, Bessie."

Bess then realized that it was a small package that her mother was carrying.

"What have you got there, Mamma?"

"Just a little something. I'll show you in a minute." She then sighed deeply. "I know, Bessie dear, that you must be fearfully disappointed that Grannie did not live long enough to give you your cristallos."

She thinks I'm mourning that. Dare she say what she was really thinking?

She took a deep breath. "Mamma, may I be perfectly honest with you?"

"Of course, dear child."

"The truth is, Mamma, I am not disappointed at all. I don't care about the daich of cristallos. I . . . I don't think I'd even make a very good glassblower." A shocked expression fled across her mother's face.

"Nonsense, Bess. Absolute nonsense. It's in our blood." Her mother's face turned pale, despite the colorful patches playing across it from the stained glass.

"But, Mamma, it might not be in mine."

Lavinia appeared even more shocked by this statement. She inhaled deeply and then spoke. Her chin was set firmly. "You shall get your daich on your sixteenth birthday. I shall give it to you. And you shall still become a fine glassmaker."

"It's not the same if you give it to me." Bess knew she shouldn't contradict her mother, but she could not help herself. Her mother's brow creased as if she was perplexed by Bess's words.

"What are you talking about? It's not the same? Just because I give this to you, rather than Grannie? Perhaps it's not exactly the same, but that doesn't matter. It's your destiny." She paused. "Your destiny!" She said the two words with force.

But what if my destiny doesn't fit? Bess thought. *Doesn't fit me, like a dress that is too big or too small? And who gets to decide what my destiny is? Why not me?* But Bess said nothing.

Lavinia Wickham shook her head gravely. "Don't deny your destiny." Bess shivered. There was almost something threatening in her mother's voice. Lavinia Wickham's face was pale, and now, with the light of a full moon pouring through a rose-colored pane, it turned a fierce red. Yes, there was an intense red color in the Wickham family's palette of glass. By adding certain minerals and compounds of salts and chemicals, they could make a particularly unique, fiery-red pigment with which to stain glass—blood fire, they called it.

"You will make a good glassblower—daich or no daich. The cristallos are still here. You will, in time, learn how to use the blowpipe, add color, create shapes. You are part of this family. You will learn!" There was a defiance in her mother's voice that Bess had never heard before.

But do I want to learn? Bess glanced at the package her mother was holding.

"What did you bring me?"

Her mother gently began to untie the strings that bound the soft cotton wadding.

"You see that?"

"Yes, a glass bunny."

"Remember the bunny you found in the garden?"

Bess shivered. "I was so excited when I first saw it! But then I realized it had been stabbed, hurt by one of those sharp petals of the Blood Thorn lilies in our glass garden . . ." She trailed off.

"Yes, and it bled to death," said her mother flatly. "The flower didn't commit murder, darling girl. We fixed up the creature a bit, and Olivia posed it beautifully. Rose drew an excellent lifelike picture of it. Then Father, with his wonderful techniques with the blowpipe, shaped it into a perfect glass replica. What do you think?"

"It's nice—I mean, lovely." She was trying not to be so contradictory, but inside, Bess was rebelling most fiercely. *But it's dead, Mamma,* she thought. *Dead as those glass flowers.*

"'Nice'? Is that all you can say? Well, young lady . . ." Bess hated it when her mother called her *young lady*. There was something so humiliating, so mocking, as if Bess was trying to be something she wasn't. "It's more than nice. It's a limited edition and has already almost sold out. It has fetched the highest price of any of our animals."

"Are you suggesting that I go on a hunt for dead animals? Because if you are, I'm not."

"Of course not. Creatures are attracted to you. Wounded ones you have brought home and patched up. They are as good as new. "

"So you want me to bring you wounded animals?" Bess could barely contain her shock.

"No, not necessarily wounded ones. But if you could just bring home some of those adorable creatures who seem to flock to you . . ." There was a little squidgy feeling in Bess's gut, as if perhaps the jam on the toast she had eaten that morning had gone moldy. She swallowed uncomfortably as her mother continued to look off into the distance and talk into the darkness of the night.

"Rose, you know, is very good at making sketches. So Olivia assisted her and rearranged its body. That's what she did with the dead bunny." Another nauseating feeling twisted in Bess's stomach as her mother continued, saying, ". . . propped it up into a hopping position."

"Mamma!" Bess gasped.

"It was dead, darling. Dead. *D-E-A-D*. It didn't feel a thing." Her voice was so soft, as if she were trying to cuddle the words. "And if Rose makes enough sketches, Father and Olivia can make excellent molds. They just need a drawing or a rendering of the creature doing what it does best. In flight if a bird, hopping if a rabbit, leaping if a deer. This is how you can contribute to the glassworks. But I promise you, Rose is so good she can catch their every movement from life. In vivo studies, they call it. And all you need to do is bring the live ones to us, where Rose can study them and sketch them."

"But where?

"Well, right here. You see, Father is thinking of building a little pen where we can keep them for just a short time while Rose sketches. And Father himself is developing some new techniques for shaping the glass that he thinks will be perfect for capturing their motion. For example, the blur of a hummingbird's wings while hovering."

"But, Mamma, hummingbirds only hover when they are gathering nectar from flowers—real flowers, not glass ones."

"We could bring one of the glass ones into the pen and dip it in honey."

"And have another dead creature on our hands? No thank you, Mamma."

"Now, don't be insolent."

Bess's face twisted into the most insolent face ever.

"Really, Bess!"

Bess was quiet for several seconds. "What would you say if I planted a garden in that pen? A real garden, with real flowers, and maybe carrots and plants that the animals could eat. They would be drawn to this garden."

"Hmmm . . ." Her mother looked doubtful as she considered the idea.

"Mamma, you know, I might make a better gardener than a glassblower."

"Nonsense, darling girl. You'll make a fine glassblower." She sighed. "But I'll discuss this with your father." She carefully wrapped up the bunny in the cotton swaddling, then bent over her daughter and gave her a good-night kiss. As she left the room, her back seemed to stiffen, and it was as if Bess could read her mind. *She's always been a difficult child. Loving but difficult. That's Bess!*

But Bess didn't care. She was so excited at the prospect of planting a garden, growing a garden with the scent of real flowers and rows upon rows of tomatoes, bunches of ruffled lettuce, and bright orange carrots. She could hardly sleep, and when she did, it was the fragrance of orange blossoms mixed with jasmine that threaded through her dreams, with colors more radiant than the palette of any glassmaker on Earth.

Later that night, Bess woke up. The entire house was very chilly since the fires had been shut down for the mourning period. The moon had slipped away to another land, and it seemed that most of the stars had followed. It was that edge of the night between the blackest of black and the first gray of dawn. She thought she heard the creak of floorboards. Was her family still up? She got out of bed and tiptoed down the ruby glass hall. She heard low voices coming from the library that held the glassmakers' books. These were books of formulas, of solutions and chemicals for staining, recipes for silica and sand and other mixtures that were essential for glassmaking.

"And you looked under Bess's bed . . . ?" Rose asked.

Bess could not hear the rest. What were they looking for under her bed? Why? What?

"Of course. That was the first place I looked," her mother said. "Right after Grannie died, before Olivia went out to tell Bess."

"When was the last time you saw it?" her father asked.

"Oh dear, I can't remember when. Maybe our wedding day."

"Wedding day? That was almost twenty years ago!" her father exploded.

"Hush, keep your voice down. I don't want Bess to hear about any of this. And besides, Bess had a good idea today.

Growing a garden to attract animals."

Bess's heart gave a little leap for joy. A garden! How she had dreamed of a real garden where flowers bloomed and unleashed fragrances, then slowly wilted with the promise to come back again. Never would they be locked into glass and become a dreadful mockery of life—false life.

"Do you suppose," Rose began to speak slowly, "that Grannie gave it to Bess before she died?"

"Traitor!" Olivia muttered. Though whispered, the word exploded in Bess's head. Had Olivia actually called their grandmother a traitor? A sadness overwhelmed her. If this was so, what might they call *her*?

There was a silence, a dreadful silence that seemed to descend through the darkness. Bess felt a terror envelop her. She felt as if she were about to be condemned. And yet she had never heard anything about this thing that they thought Grannie had given to her. She crept back to her bedroom. That last word she'd heard, *traitor*, echoed in her brain. And that word felt like a knife. She felt as if she had been cut and was bleeding.

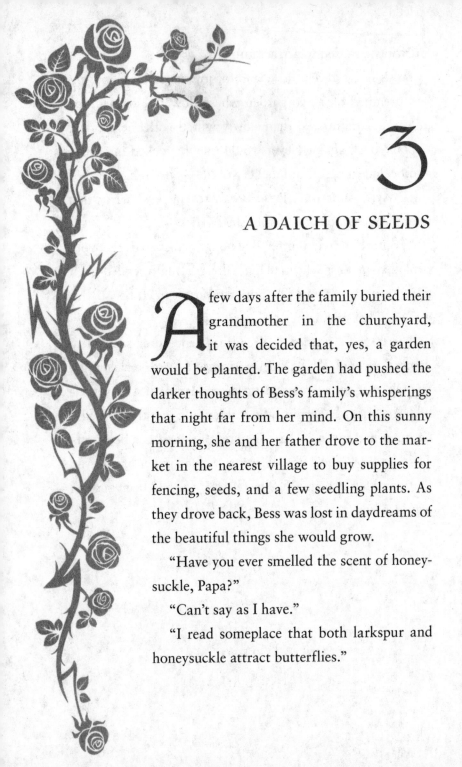

3

A DAICH OF SEEDS

A few days after the family buried their grandmother in the churchyard, it was decided that, yes, a garden would be planted. The garden had pushed the darker thoughts of Bess's family's whisperings that night far from her mind. On this sunny morning, she and her father drove to the market in the nearest village to buy supplies for fencing, seeds, and a few seedling plants. As they drove back, Bess was lost in daydreams of the beautiful things she would grow.

"Have you ever smelled the scent of honeysuckle, Papa?"

"Can't say as I have."

"I read someplace that both larkspur and honeysuckle attract butterflies."

"Umm." Her father sounded rather bored. But she went on.

"Honeysuckle is a lovely vine. We could grow it right by our back door. It would make a beautiful decoration."

"Humph." Her father made the sound he often did that usually indicated mild disapproval.

"I think you'd like them, Papa," Bess said, her voice tinted with eagerness. Just a hint, however. It never paid to get too enthusiastic about anything with her father.

"Do they attract hummingbirds as well as butterflies?" he asked.

"Yes, most definitely, Papa."

"Hadn't you said there was a place in the forest where there are—what do you call a group of hummingbirds?"

"A charm, Papa. A group of hummingbirds is called a charm." Bess always loved that word. "But they are very flighty creatures. Never settle down for more than a split second." She remembered the ruby-throated hummingbird that had danced in front of her like a liquid flame. "But maybe they would, if I grew enough honeysuckle and larkspur and lupine and columbine."

"We might be able to get as many orders for hummingbird figurines as we did for the rabbit. No other glassmakers make them." He paused, then added, "I'd make a limited edition, of course. That drives the price up on each one. And I would imagine that there are more varieties of hummingbirds than there are rabbits."

17

"Oh, many more, Papa. Hundreds, I believe."

"Hundreds!" he exclaimed with delight.

"Oh yes. There's the purple-throated woodstar, and the violet-tailed sylph, and the tourmaline sunangel, and the crowned woodnymph—so beautiful, with emerald-green feathers on its head that blend into sapphire-blue plumage on its body. Airborne jewels, they are!"

"My dear, you have just described a fortune, a wealth of possibilities."

How odd, Bess thought. *He thinks of wealth, and I think of blessings—airborne blessings, fleeting but all the more miraculous.*

He shifted the reins to one hand, then pressed his nose to Bess's head, with its thick, auburn-colored braid.

"Bess, I've always said that your hair looks like dark honey and smells like nectar. That's how you draw small creatures to you."

Bess clamped her eyes shut. When her father did this, she always wanted to say, *I'm not bait, Papa. It's not my hair. It's that I have learned their ways.* She felt somehow that her family had never really understood her. She felt different in ways she could not exactly understand herself. They drove on for another mile or so.

"Look, dear child, I can see the everlasting roses from here."

"Yes," Bess replied sullenly.

"It's really a favorite for graves. So many orders came after your grandmother was buried. The ones we made for the top of her grave have become our bestseller. We are calling them the Remembrance Bouquet. Low to the ground, so the wind won't break them. Clever, eh?" He paused and then blurted out, "Look ahead, dear, to the glass house. I see smoke coming from the chimneys. Bless her heart. Your mamma has started up the fires again. I'm sure your grannie would approve."

"Really?"

"Of course she would."

An idea suddenly came to her. "Papa, could we stop at the graveyard?"

"Why would you want to do that?"

"I just remembered the seedling violet plants we bought. I might plant some on Grannie's grave . . ."

"But they don't last."

"But they spread, and they'll come back in the spring."

Her father shook his head. "If that's what you want to do." He sighed. "Your mother and I were thinking of making a glass bouquet for spring. Glass bouquets that could be changed for each season."

"I suppose that would be nice, too," she replied dully as her father drew the cart to a halt by the graveyard gates. She hopped down and carried a flat of the violet plants to the gravesite.

The ground had hardened since the burial, and she tried her best to scrape at it with her hands. Finally, she took off her shoe, which had a good, sturdy heel on it, and gouged at the earth. The soil loosened. She dug a shallow hole that was just deep enough for a violet plant's short roots. She quickly dug three more holes. She knew that if she tended the violets they would spread, and she envisioned a quilt of them over the grave. She might even add some more flowers and seeds. In time, it might look like a patchwork quilt of flowers. She felt happy. As she got up from the ground and dusted off her skirt, she murmured, "I'll be back, Grannie. I'll be back."

A short time later, they turned onto the drive up to the glass house. There was a sudden burst of sunshine. It was as if a spectrum of color had shattered into shards, as blades of light sliced through tinted glass and scattered across the land.

"Time for my specs," her father muttered, then turned toward Bess. The dark circles of glass peered at her. It was almost as if he became another person. Not Papa. "Don't know how you do it, Bess. Going without specs."

"I guess I'm just different," she whispered. *But I'm not a traitor! Nor was Grannie.*

"What did you say?"

"Nothing, Papa. Nothing."

She looked ahead at the mammoth house with its glass shingles and chimneys and twisting spires—all of it made from crystals forged in the ovens of the Wickhams, who had settled in this valley long, long ago. Some said the Wickhams were there in the time of the druids, that they had learned their magic with glass from those ancient Celtic priests. But were they priests or magicians? What were the Wickhams exactly—glassblowers or sorcerers?

"Your grannie didn't need the specs, either." He paused. "You're alike in that way."

"Am I?"

"Indeed, lass."

So at least she was like someone in her family. Had Grannie felt like her, then? That she somehow didn't belong? Had been born into the wrong family?

"Oh, good," her father said as they drove through the gates. "The fires are back up completely. Mourning is over." He must have felt Bess wince, for he turned to her and patted her knee. "Officially over, but we'll keep her close in our hearts." He sighed. "You know, dear, it never pays to drag these things out. It's unnatural."

Bess followed her father into the glass studio. Her mother stood in front of the box that was the main oven. The hole in the side of the oven was where she put the glass that had already been melted in the "gathering" oven. She withdrew the long rod of the pipe, which now had a spherical blob on the end. While resting the rod at an angle on a flat stone surface, she blew softly through the blowpipe. She needed to keep twirling it so it would not sag or develop any flat spots. In the meantime, Rose came from the gathering oven with another blob that she would transfer to the top of her mother's spherical one, which had now been inflated to the proper oval for the body of the rabbit. This new, smaller sphere would be the head. With tongs, Lavinia Wickham began to pull it into the small oval shape of a rabbit's head. Then she reinserted the body of the rabbit with the head attached into the oven, all while continuing to twirl it. This way the shape would not sag and completely collapse, and at the same time would become more pliable, so that continuous shaping could be done.

"You want me to get some bits, Mamma, from the gathering oven?" Bess asked.

"No need. I think I have enough here on the head to pull the ears out."

With the tongs, Lavinia had pulled two stubby ears from the top of the rabbit's head as Bess watched. Then it went back into the oven again. "Last pull, I think," Lavinia said. When she withdrew it the next time, she pulled the ears out several more inches. "Quick, the duckbill shears, Rose."

The two girls watched as their mother began to expertly cut the excess molten glass into perfect replicas of a rabbit's long, tapering ears.

"There we go! Now to the cooling oven." Lavinia snipped the glass rabbit from the rod for the transfer to the cooling oven.

"Almost perfect!" Lavinia sighed.

These two words—*almost perfect*—were uttered aloud after every piece they made, even though they were considered among the finest glassmakers in England. They were members of the Union of Saint Nicholas, the patron saint of glassmakers, and very few glassblowers in England were selected to belong to this guild. Most were from Italy and Germany. The Saint Nicholas was the most elite of all trade guilds.

However, Lavinia and her husband, Charles, never seemed satisfied. If a piece was declared perfect, it could be submitted to the board of the guild to receive the Maker's Mark. No glassmaker in England had ever received that designation. Only two living artists in the entire world had received the Maker's Mark, and those glass artists were both in Murano, Italy. Before, there had been more. People now blamed it on the quality of the cristallos. But the Wickham family was determined to earn their Maker's Mark, and it was often a topic at the dinner table.

Bess looked at the scraps in the bucket that had been cut from the molten glass to make the ears. This was something she could never do. But if it would give her a chance to grow a garden, that would be wonderful. And she did like catching little animals for Rose to draw. She always kept the pictures. For her, the drawings were actually more lifelike than the glass figurines. In some way, those crystal figurines seemed to lock the animal in a cold eternity. Odd that she would use the word *cold*, even though they were created in fires of unimaginable heat.

That night she went to bed the happiest she had been since Grannie had died. All she could think about was the garden she would plant tomorrow. There would be rows of radishes. Bunnies loved radishes and cabbages, and birds loved seeds, so she would be sure to scatter some about. She would get some more seeds the next time she went to the village. She fell asleep dreaming of columbine, their star-shaped outer petals and delicate throats tipped up, as if expecting a hummingbird to come for its nectar.

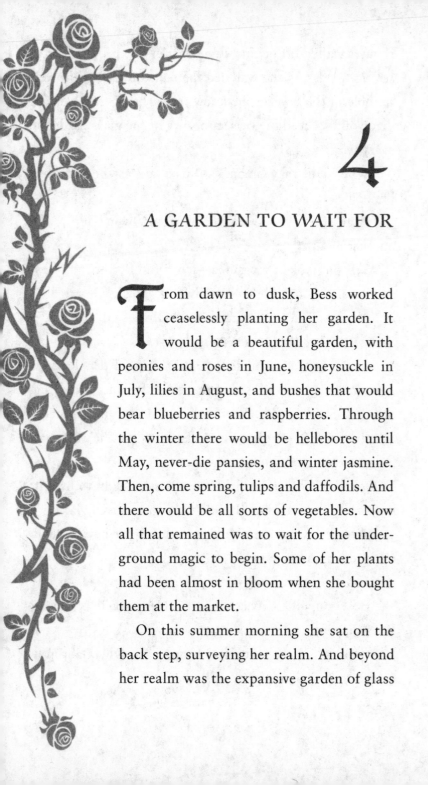

4

A GARDEN TO WAIT FOR

From dawn to dusk, Bess worked ceaselessly planting her garden. It would be a beautiful garden, with peonies and roses in June, honeysuckle in July, lilies in August, and bushes that would bear blueberries and raspberries. Through the winter there would be hellebores until May, never-die pansies, and winter jasmine. Then, come spring, tulips and daffodils. And there would be all sorts of vegetables. Now all that remained was to wait for the underground magic to begin. Some of her plants had been almost in bloom when she bought them at the market.

On this summer morning she sat on the back step, surveying her realm. And beyond her realm was the expansive garden of glass flowers walled off behind stone barriers, to protect it from strong winds. As she watched the buds of her real flowers tremble in the breeze, she knew in her heart that her garden would exceed the perfect beauty of the glass garden in every way.

"When will they bloom?" Olivia said as she sat down beside Bess.

"Well, these honeysuckle blossoms won't open for another month."

"Yes, but look at my spirea—it's in full flower."

"It's always in full flower, Olivia. It's glass."

"Always. That's the beauty of it," Olivia said.

That's what cheapens it, Bess thought.

"And . . ." Olivia added, "there's a big order. Princess Alinda, the second cousin of the king of France, is getting married. She's French. Very stylish. And she has specially asked for one of my glass bouquets. Imagine! She's heard of my glass bouquets from across the sea."

Just the Channel—hardly a sea, Bess thought to herself, but kept her mouth shut. It didn't pay to anger Olivia.

"She even wants a rosebud wreath for her hair." Olivia clapped her hands in glee.

"And a glass wedding dress as well?" Bess asked.

"How stupid!" Olivia sneered. "Next you'll be saying glass slippers."

A pool of silence seemed to form. Then Olivia abruptly turned to her younger sister.

"So, when will the fun begin? When will all the dear little creatures flock here?"

"Soon, I hope, and when the flowers begin to bloom, I'll keep a sharp lookout for them."

"Where would you go to find our models?" Olivia asked.

Models, she calls them! So very cold. A chill ran down Bess's spine.

"Uh . . . I guess in the forest, where the hummingbirds gather in their charms. I'd introduce them to the fragrance of a few flowers."

"And they'll follow you back here?"

"I hope so, maybe." But she felt something darken within her.

Olivia tipped her head. "You do have your uses, little sister."

Then she left abruptly.

Uses. The word burned in Bess's ears like acid, and the conversation from that night echoed in her mind. *Even though I might be a "traitor," like Grannie?*

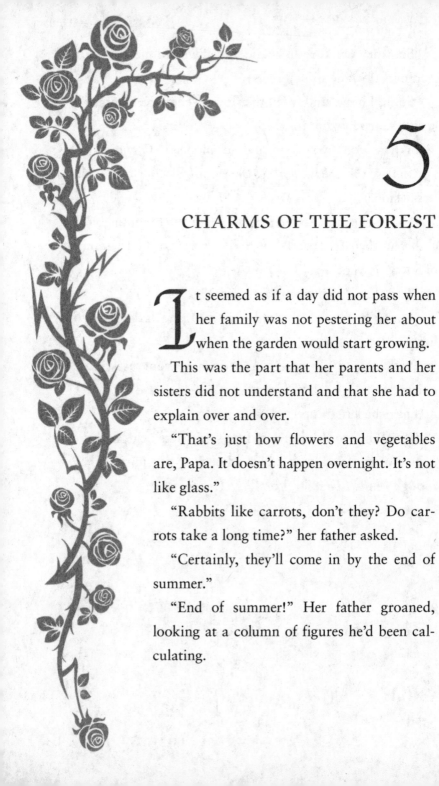

5

CHARMS OF THE FOREST

It seemed as if a day did not pass when her family was not pestering her about when the garden would start growing. This was the part that her parents and her sisters did not understand and that she had to explain over and over.

"That's just how flowers and vegetables are, Papa. It doesn't happen overnight. It's not like glass."

"Rabbits like carrots, don't they? Do carrots take a long time?" her father asked.

"Certainly, they'll come in by the end of summer."

"End of summer!" Her father groaned, looking at a column of figures he'd been calculating.

His wife peered over his shoulder. "Those bunnies were a gold mine," she muttered.

Her father looked up. "But Bess tells me that hummingbirds have many more species. I mean, rabbits—they come in what colors?"

Come in . . . The words irritated Bess mightily.

"I s'pose mostly brown or tan or white, maybe gray." Her father sighed after answering his own question.

"But, Papa, rabbits aren't manufactured. They're born."

"Well, no matter. Bess, dear, tell your mother all the kinds of hummingbirds there are—as many colors as the rainbow."

"Er . . . uh . . ." Bess was uncomfortable.

It felt as if the words, the names of the hummingbirds, were stuck inside her. "Well . . . uh, there's the ruby-throated hummingbird . . . and the fiery topaz."

"Fiery topaz," her mother repeated softly, stroking her own throat.

"And the azure-crowned hummingbird and the blue-headed sapphire."

"Oh my goodness." Her mother pressed a hand to her bodice as if she were about to swoon. "So dazzling. We could make dozens of limited editions." She rejoiced, took out a piece of paper, and began making calculations. A few minutes later she looked up at Bess. "Do you realize that if we could make limited editions of a mere dozen species . . .

we could bring in over one thousand pounds sterling? And you say there are hundreds of species?"

"Yes, Mamma."

A dread was building deep in Bess's gut.

"I think you need to go out right now to that forest where the charms live."

"Now? But it's raining."

"So what?"

"They never come out in the rain. Rain dulls the scent of the flowers with the nectar they seek, Mamma."

But within seconds the rain stopped, and as the sun came out, like a clash of silent cymbals, colors crashed through the thousands upon thousands of glass panes of the glass house.

Lavinia Wickham put on her dark round spectacles. And in an instant, her pursed lips drew into the slash of a smile. "Not now, darling. It's sunny! Go out and seek a humming-bird. I am longing for a ruby-throated one." And again, she caressed her long, elegant neck.

I am so different from them—all of them. Freakishly different, Bess thought. However, what could she do but obey her parents? So she set out, taking a shortcut to the sur-rounding woods, and within minutes she was in a place quite the opposite of the glass garden. It was a true forest, redolent with the scent of trees and moss, the music of creeks, and the quiet wonders of life. It was where the dear creatures that Bess loved dwelled. They all came to her unbidden. Her only lure was her quietness. She would settle down and keep very still, and sooner or later a nearby mouse, a rabbit, or an adorable baby hedgehog, all prickly and roly-poly, would appear.

Today, however, she headed to a far corner of the woods—the hummingbird grove. The trees had begun to thin, and, looking up, she knew she had arrived. The air was suddenly strung with tiny glittering missiles. Humming-birds. She settled quietly on a mossy mound, with a few stems of wild woodland flowers she had picked on her way. Looking up, she saw what appeared to be a sparkling web of jewels—darting jewels. It was magical. She caught sight of one hovering high above her head. It had emerald-green feathers and a rose-pink throat. She felt her own heart begin to beat wildly. She knew the bird was preparing to dive. *Flying jewelry!* Bess thought, and no sooner had the two words formed in her mind than the creature alighted on her knee. Its tail was still vibrating, and these vibrations were a language of their own. The languages of creatures came naturally to Bess. Had since she was a child. And so Bess made soft *brrrr* sounds that were a response—a response that no human would ever be able to comprehend.

"You want me to come to see your new chicks? What? One's not hatched yet?"

The hummingbird flew up to Bess's cheek and brushed it with her left wing.

"Yes? That's a yes?"

She rose up and followed the emerald glimmer through the woods to a birch tree. The nest was nearly at the top, but Bess, an expert tree climber, made a quick business of it.

"Ahh," she sighed, as she peered down into the nest made of dandelion down, spider silk, and moss. Two tiny mouths opened. The chicks were no bigger than half the tip of a pinkie finger. The unhatched egg was the size of a jellybean. It began to rock just slightly.

"It's coming . . . it's coming . . ." the mother hummingbird squeaked.

"It will be hungry," Bess said. She knew that the mother would have to make at least one hundred trips a day to gather food for the hatched chicks.

"Indeed! Three of them to feed!" replied the hummingbird.

"I brought these flowers, but go out now and gather some more nectar. I'll stay here. I even have my eyedropper, so I can feed them nectar from the ones I brought."

"You're a blessing, Bess." The hummingbird sighed.

Half an hour later, Bess climbed back down the tree. No sooner had her feet touched the ground than another hummingbird appeared.

"Stellina!" she exclaimed. "So good to see you, and not tangled in a spider's web."

"Ah, Bess, you got me out of that, and now that same silk is in my nest."

"Where it rightfully belongs. Any eggs yet?"

"Not yet, but maybe soon. Should we fly together for a bit?"

Bess giggled. She loved that the hummingbirds referred to her walking as flying. It felt as if they had folded her into their charm.

They "flew" for several minutes while Bess pondered quietly to herself. *Should I lead her to the new garden? Should I ask her to pose or not?* The question hung in her mind for a good long time. Finally, she got up her nerve.

"Would you consider, Stellina, doing me a favor?"

"Anything, dear, anything. I owe my life to you."

And so she explained about the garden and how her parents would like Stellina to pose for a glass sculpture, and that very soon there would be a full garden blooming with delicious nectar. "How lovely," Stellina said. For one could always use nectar, especially if planning a family. She swooped up in delight to where the canopy opened to the sky, revealing a patch of blue. Bess tipped her head back and watched the glittering ruby-throated hummingbird dive and twirl like a tiny, feathered asteroid. It was as if she owned the sky.

A few minutes later, Bess knocked on the door of the glass house. "Mamma, I'm home."

Lavinia Wickham opened the door. She was wearing her dark round glasses as she peered at the beautiful creature perched on her daughter's shoulder. Stellina felt an odd twinge in her tiny gizzard.

"I'll take the lovely bird from here," Lavinia said, and wrapped her hand around the tiny creature.

6

AN OWL IS CURSED

The three Wickham daughters were in the vegetable garden that had grown robustly since Bess had planted it. "Olivia, are you sure that you freed that little rabbit last night?"

"Yes, why would you doubt me?"

"Why would I doubt you? Because the food bowl is still untouched. I had left perfect bunny food for it, parsley and mint and cut-up carrots." If Bess had not looked up, she would not have seen the dark glances exchanged by Olivia and Rose.

"Perhaps it wasn't hungry?" Rose said.

Now Bess began to wonder about the hummingbird, Stellina, too. She had told her parents to release any hummingbirds through the west cupola, so they could catch the best breezes for flight. But had she ever seen one leave? Maybe once—a fiery topaz that had proven most ornery and given Rose a solid peck on her nose that she called "disfiguring." But Rose had a tendency to exaggerate.

Then a vile curse slashed through the bright sunshine. It was their father, Charles Wickham, high up in a turret, waving his arms madly at an owl. *"Mallachd air do sgiathan!"* he roared in old Celt, the language of their ancestors.

"A druid curse," Olivia whispered. "He shouldn't have."

"Why not?" Bess said, tilting her head.

"A druid curse against an owl," Olivia whispered. "It could bring bad luck. Evil creatures, they are, full of dark magic."

"Nonsense," Bess whispered to herself. This was a most beautiful creature. Its heart-shaped face blazed white, as did its chest feathers—white with dark speckles. The rest of its feathers were tawny. Its wingspan was almost as wide as her father was tall. Suddenly the owl folded its wings and plunged down. Rose and Olivia fell to the ground, screeching and cowering with their hands over their heads. But Bess stood tall, mesmerized by the owl, its black eyes like dark mirrors, so shiny she could see her own reflection. The leading edge of its wings brushed her cheek gently. Then it rose, instantly gaining height. Higher and higher it went and appeared to dissolve into the cumulus of a white cloud.

"It attacked you!" Rose screamed.

"It did no such thing!" Bess snapped.

"Papa should never have cursed it."

"Don't be silly!"

"It tried to bite you," Olivia said.

"Nonsense. Its wing just brushed my face. It was not a bite at all . . . it . . . it was soft and silky." She was tempted to say *like a kiss*. But of course, she had never been kissed, and that was sure to bring a mocking response from her two sisters.

Within minutes, their father stomped into the garden. He was carrying a gun.

"Papa! No!" Bess said.

"The cursed bird attacked you."

"No, not at all."

"He's a nosy creature. He's been flying around here for days."

"You know, Bess, maybe that owl is the culprit that snatched the rabbit you set the bowl out for," Olivia said.

A light kindled in her father's eyes. "Absolutely!"

"Yes, yes . . . the owl must be the culprit. I believe I saw the bird take a hummingbird the other day, and that barn cat," Rose offered.

"One of our bestsellers," their father said.

At that moment their mother came out.

"What's all the fuss about?" she asked. "And, Charles, why are you out here with a gun?"

"We think, Lavinia, that we've found our thief."

"Thief?" Lavinia said.

"You know how some of the animals simply disappear. Usually, we can see that they've eaten the charming little meals Bess puts out for them. But occasionally . . ." Her father paused.

It was in that moment that Bess knew her family was lying. All of them were looking at her expectantly. The question in their eyes was all the same—*Does she believe us?*

And the answer was, *NO!*

7

PIERCED

"Here you go, little fella." Her mother crouched over the baby red fox, where she had set down a pan of milk. "Off you go to your mammy. She'll be waiting for you by the birch grove." The kit stuck its tongue out and lapped up the milk.

"I'll take him, Mamma; he might not know the way."

"Well, you tell his mamma that the little fellow did splendidly."

"Oh, good. Can I see the figurine when I come back?"

There was a sudden glare in her mother's eyes. A glare of panic. "Well, it's still in the cooling oven, of course. And as you know, accidents can happen during cooling."

"Yes, of course."

This is a conversation of lies, Bess thought. And that was how it had been for the last several days. A great show of releasing the creatures—food set out, her sisters waving goodbye as the creatures hopped, crawled, or flew. The release ceremonies became more elaborate. A nectar recipe that Bess had mixed up and set in a bright red bowl. Then there was the timothy hay sprinkled with grains for bunnies and squirrels.

And yet none of this eased Bess's worries. Too many creatures had simply disappeared. What had happened to that first hummingbird she had brought—the ruby-throated one? Stellina. Mamma had promised to release Stellina the next morning. Bess could have done it, but they had sent her off to market at dawn. Stellina had been building a nest in the forest for when she would lay her eggs. Had that ever happened?

Every day Bess's suspicions grew.

Finally, one night, something stirred her in her sleep. She touched her cheek exactly where the owl's wing had touched her, perhaps a month ago. She woke up suddenly and stared into the blackness of the night. The moon was not full but just bright enough to cast slices and slivers of colored light through the highest windows in her bedroom. It wasn't a rainbow, but a night bow, as her grannie had called these dancing lights that often appeared in the glass house. Her grannie's voice came back to her: "You know, dearie, they say that at the end of the rainbow there is treasure to be found."

"Yes, Grannie," she had replied.

"Well, at the end of a night bow, something better can be found."

"What's that, Grannie?"

"A blessing."

"Not a pot of gold?"

"No. A blessing."

"What kind of a blessing?"

"Well, that is for you to find out. I can't predict what kind of blessing you might find. But sometimes it takes a bit of courage, you know."

Drafty winds wrapped around the glass house. It was certainly not a night to go out, but perhaps she would find this blessing. So she put on her heaviest shawl and pulled a hat down over her ears, then laced up her boots.

The moon was larger than she had thought, and it cast a patchwork swirl of muted color on the fields surrounding the glass house. She was drawn for some reason to the walled glass garden. She opened the gate and began to walk through the daylilies. Their glass blossoms "bloomed" all through the night, and the scentless roses clambered over a trellis. She paused to look at a thicket of foxglove. Each one's blossom reminded her of a speckled throat tipped up. But to catch what? The evening moonlight? The morning sun? No, nothing. This silly garden seemed to Bess to be deader than dead.

And then, as if to underscore her thoughts, her eyes opened wide in horror. She heard a foreign sound, a soft gasping. Directly ahead there was a gruesome sight. A sight that she could not exactly sort out in her mind. The blossoms were red, bloodred, and the needles were sharp. And there, hanging from the needles, was the owl she had seen. The owl her father had cursed and threatened to shoot now hung bleeding from the Blood Thorn lilies. Its white-speckled breast feathers were drenched in blood.

She gasped in horror and rushed to the bird. Dropping to her knees, she tried to soothe it. "Hush . . . hush . . ." she purred, and then began to hum a sort of lullaby. Delicately, she began to remove the bird from the deadly thorns that had snagged it in flight. Her own hands were soon bleeding, but she did not care. She began speaking a language that she thought the owl would perhaps understand.

"Almost free . . . almost free," she whispered. The owl blinked and opened his dark eyes wide. There was a kindling light in them. "You are the blessing," the owl gasped. Bess thought, *Yes, he understands me.* As soon as he was free, Bess wrapped the owl carefully in her shawl. She glanced toward the glass house. It seemed in this moment to glow with the fire of the furnaces. In the past, she had taken injured animals home to recover, but not now. *Never,* she thought. Not with her suspicions of her family.

She knew there was an abandoned hedgehog nest in a hollow log in the forest. She would take the owl there. It was near a wolf lair. The two wolves and their pups who lived in this lair trusted her. She had found one of their pups when it had wandered away, and learned their names, Lear and Jenig. They would look out for the owl. She was certain. Often, they brought her bloody bits of meat from their prey. She never ate the bits, of course, making endless excuses, but finally explaining that she could not eat raw meat. The wolves were struck with disbelief. "But why?" they had asked. "I'm human," Bess had begun to explain. The wolves blinked. "I have a human stomach."

"Human. What's that?" the father asked.

"It's not wolf," she had replied.

The she-wolf came closer and peered into Bess's green eyes, so close in color to her own and those of her mate. "I'm not wolf," Bess repeated. "Human—just human." The wolf family accepted her but were never completely convinced that she was not wolf.

The wolves insisted that she bring the injured bird right into their lair, a shallow cave under the overhang of a cliff. They watched as Bess began to unravel her knitted shawl and bind the chest wounds on the owl. This was after soaking up the blood with sphagnum moss to stop the bleeding and prevent infection. Her grannie had told her about this "wonder cure," as she called it. She had explained that many of these cures had come from the druids. Whenever Lavinia heard Grannie say this, she would mutter, "Witchcraft nonsense," and scurry out of the kitchen. Grannie would just snort. "Your mamma would have lost that hand she burned when she was learning to take glass off the blowpipe if I hadn't bound it in sphagnum."

"Bry, bry," Bess soothed the owl.

"You are speaking owl to him, Bess?" the wolf asked.

"Yes. I'm sure you will, too, very soon, and he'll speak wolf to you as well." Creatures were remarkable in picking up other animals' languages, gestures, and codes, no matter if one had feathers and the other fur, or one had teeth and the other a beak and talons.

Of course, the best thing was that owls ate raw meat. So the wolf family could hunt for their patient. And they were as keen and skillful hunters on land as owls were in the air.

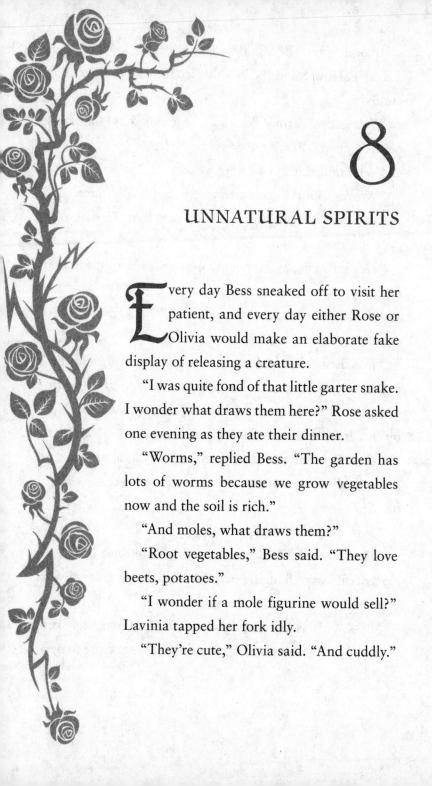

8

UNNATURAL SPIRITS

Every day Bess sneaked off to visit her patient, and every day either Rose or Olivia would make an elaborate fake display of releasing a creature.

"I was quite fond of that little garter snake. I wonder what draws them here?" Rose asked one evening as they ate their dinner.

"Worms," replied Bess. "The garden has lots of worms because we grow vegetables now and the soil is rich."

"And moles, what draws them?"

"Root vegetables," Bess said. "They love beets, potatoes."

"I wonder if a mole figurine would sell?" Lavinia tapped her fork idly.

"They're cute," Olivia said. "And cuddly."

"Not in glass," Bess said with an edge. She looked around the table. How could she be so different from the rest of her family?

"You know, Farmer Buckham down the road had a raid on his pigpen," Bess's father said.

"Who raided it?" asked her mother.

"Wolves. But the good news is he shot one of them."

Bess's hand began to tremble so hard that she had to set the soup spoon down.

"He's bringing it over here and we'll try out our taxidermy."

"You're going to stuff a dead wolf?" Bess gasped in disbelief.

"Just the head, my dear. They're cutting it off and sending it over. But we are also going to make a glass casting of it. It will be a big seller, I know." Lavinia Wickham put out her hand as if to warn her husband not to say anything more. As Bess listened, the room began to spin. She emitted an unintelligible string of words and slumped forward in her chair.

"She's possessed!" Olivia said.

When she came to her senses, she was in her bed. Both her parents were hanging over her, their faces creased with concern.

"Bess . . . Bess . . . you're awake now?" her mother asked.

"My Lord." Charles Wickham drew his face close to hers.

"What could have set you off? What were you gabbling about?"

"Gabbling?" she whispered.

"Yes, dear," her mother said. "Speaking in some language we've never heard."

"Oh, oh . . . I don't know."

"It was as if you were seized by some . . . some unnatural spirit," her father said. Her mother shot him a darting glance.

Unnatural spirit . . . Two words from the witch-burning times in England. Fear now flooded through Bess. Surely her parents didn't believe she was a witch. She knew what she had said now. She had spoken in wolf. But she could hardly say this to her parents.

She would wait until it grew darker, then she would sneak out of the house. She needed to go to the wolves. Was it the father or mother, or one of their pups who had been killed?

Like a dark ribbon of sound, the mournful howling streamed through the woods as she made her way through the moonless night to get as far away as possible from the glass house. Finally, she crumpled over, dropping to her knees as the keening wrapped around her and the words of the baying wolves began to make sense. "Lear, Lear, Lear, our friend is dead." A growl of despair and anger erupted from her throat. *Who am I? What am I? I belong nowhere. Wild and human, I am caught between two worlds.*

She sank into a deep sleep, unbothered by cold or the rain that began to fall. She finally stirred just before dawn, as she felt something soft brush her cheek. It was a familiar sensation. She opened her eyes slowly. The white heart-shaped face was inches from her own.

"Owl, is it you? You have recovered. You are flying again?"

"Most certainly. My name is Ulli. And you?"

"Bess," she said softly. "Just Bess."

9

THE DARK SECRETS
OF A GLASS HOUSE

"So, you see, Bess, because of you and the wolves, I'm fully recovered. But yes, I'm sorry, Lear, our friend, was the wolf who the farmer killed."

Bess had vowed she would not let any of the wolves of Lear's family know about the grotesque plans for Lear's head. Indeed, if she ever saw that glass head, she would smash it into pieces. Jenig, his partner, mewled in a corner, and both her cubs had crawled up onto Bess's lap.

"Believe me, it's better than what happened to the others," Ulli said.

"The others?" Bess asked.

"The other creatures who became figurines locked in glass."

Bess felt something quake inside her.

"Are they all dead?" But she knew they must be. Her suspicions, her hunches, had come true.

"Perhaps not exactly," Ulli replied.

"I don't understand."

"That day that your father tried to shoot me. That was not the first day that I had flown over the chimneys, the ovens, the hot shop of the glassworks. After your grannie died, I had observed many times that they began to practice some ancient forging techniques from the time of the druids. These were forbidden, as they were unnatural and perverse. Have you ever heard the term *anam tharraing*?"

Bess shook her head.

"It means the extraction of the soul." A shiver went down Bess's spine.

"The creature is fed an ominous brew of melted crystals sweetened with honey. The animal quickly becomes addled and loses its bearings. If it's a frog, it might hop backward or sideways. Jump up when it means to go down. Similarly with a bird, a hummingbird, perhaps." Bess began to feel a retching in her stomach. "They surround the creature with mirrors. Handblown glass mirrors. It becomes confused and finally smashes into the mirrors, which then break. This is the sign that the soul has been extracted. Has shattered. Then your sisters piece the fragments together following the sketches Rose made of the creature when it was alive. Then the fragments are melted down in the gathering oven and transferred to a blowpipe, and the figurine is formed. Or 'reborn,' as they say."

"They say!" Bess echoed in a scalding voice.

"Yes, dead, but a perfect figurine of what it had once been. No tools, no shears, no pincers or tongs needed for cutting or twisting. The figure that emerges is the soul of the animal itself. It is the darkest of the old druid dark arts."

"It's done with dark mirrors," Bess whispered. They were forbidden. How had her family come to possess them? Was this the thing—the gift—her family thought Grannie had saved for her?

Bess's eyes opened wide as she envisioned this horror. She then closed her eyes and imagined those glass souls, trapped like some macabre parade of animals. Not just glass souls but lost souls. For where would there be a heaven for glass souls? Nowhere. The souls captured in glass would reside in homes, in palaces, in libraries and salons of rich people, until a servant broke one when dusting or a child in a tantrum picked up a rabbit and smashed it on the floor. So what, then, would happen to the wolf's head made from poor Lear, her friend from the forest?

Bess was silent for a long time. The wolves had stopped their mewling and turned their attention to Bess. Jenig got up from the floor of the cave, came to Bess's side, and licked her cheek. Bess buried her face in the thick, soft fur of Jenig's neck. Finally, she pulled away from the mother wolf. She looked directly at Ulli. "I will never go home again."

Bess continued looking into the dark eyes of the owl, then turned toward the wolves—Jenig and the two little pups, Alva and Amor. It came to her quickly—

This is my family now. I love them. I trust them.
And I no longer trust my own.

Part Two

THE WAND

10

VOICES IN THE NIGHT

On the third night that Bess slept in the cave with the wolves, she thought she heard voices calling—familiar voices, her father and sisters! The wolves slept on, but she jerked awake and saw that Ulli the owl was also awake.

"It's them!" she whispered.

Ulli nodded. "I'll go out and see."

"No, Ulli, Papa might have a gun." *And*, she thought, *how he would love to shoot you and do what he did to poor Lear—cast you in glass.*

"You told me how superstitious humans are about owls. I'll scare him off," Ulli replied.

"Don't go. It's not worth the risk," Bess pleaded. But Ulli would not listen to her. He was off before she could say another word.

She sat trembling in the cave. Suddenly Jenig was awake.

"What is it?" she whispered. The pups who had been sleeping by her side stirred.

"We heard voices. Ulli went out to see."

"I'm going," Jenig announced, and bounded out of the cave.

"No, no, don't go. What if there's a gun . . . ?" But she couldn't finish the sentence before the wolf was gone.

The pups began to mewl.

"Hush . . . hush . . ." Bess gathered them close to her, wrapping them in the tattered shawl she had used to bind Ulli's wounds. She pressed them to her chest. She could hear footsteps coming closer. There were voices she recognized.

"Follow me, girls."

"Papa, it's so dark."

"What if there are wolves?" Rose said, thinking of the beautiful glass wolf's head they had cast that morning.

Charles Wickham inhaled sharply as a luminous green emanated through the darkness. "Impossible!" he muttered, his musket ready.

"What's impossible, Papa?"

A loud crack split the air and the scent of gunpowder wafted through the trees.

"No! It's that wolf! His soul! The soul is unleashed," Charles Wickham screamed.

And in the cave, tears ran down Bess's face. Something

had been killed out there. One shot and a life had ended. Was it Ulli or Jenig?

Was it seconds, or minutes, or an hour that passed? Time became meaningless. And then at last Jenig bounded into the cave, followed by Ulli.

Bess blinked and crumpled with relief.

"He thought I was Lear," Jenig said. "When I stepped from the brush, he thought I was the ghost of Lear."

"The soul of Lear," Ulli added. "Coming back to haunt him." The owl then turned toward Bess. "I think, dear Bess, even though we gave them a good scare, we must move deeper into the woods to be safe."

"Really?"

"They are greedy and want more. I heard your sisters talking about finding the forest of charms. They are planning to set out with butterfly nets to capture the hummingbirds." Bess closed her eyes. And for the thousandth time, she wondered what kind of family she had been born into. Had her grannie ever been like this? Impossible!

She turned to Ulli. "Before we go deeper into the forest, I must visit my grannie's grave."

"Are you sure, dear?" Jenig said. "It could be dangerous."

"Not if I go now. They are too frightened to go out right now, since you scared them." She smiled a bit. "They will still be worried about the ghost of Lear."

"But the hoarfrost is coming."

"Exactly—it's the right time. When the trees bleed white

with frost and every limb and pine needle is shrouded in ice, it is said that the hoar spirits come like ghosts from the frost, in the night. And it is then I want to visit my grannie's grave. Perhaps I can feel her spirit one last time."

Outside, snow had begun to fall. Stepping out of the cave, Bess looked north toward the low mountains that she could glimpse through the trees. She knew she must wait until water droplets suspended in those mountains began to form mist and fog on the trees. Then the mist would turn the trees into sweeps of flying ghosts encrusted with hoarfrost. Grannie had called it the time of the rime, when freezing water vapor combined with what seemed like magic. It would sculpt the ghostly spirits of trees—the souls of trees—into figures. A poem her grannie had once recited to her on a hoarfrost evening now sang in her head.

> *In the time of the rime*
> *When the droplets fall*
> *Come the spirits of the cold*
> *Like dancing souls*
> *'Tween heaven and earth*
> *Like ghosts of spirits*
> *Unleashed.*
> *They fly, they spring,*
> *They leap and bound*

Without a trace nor whisper of sound
Under the grace of the moon's light
they are souls of this silvered night.

As the frost, or rime, formed, a new luminescence filtered through the darkness of the night. Bess bundled herself into her shawl, wrapped her hands in thick patches of moss for warmth, and set out toward the church graveyard where her grannie now rested.

The frost had transformed everything as she approached the church. The gravestones in the cemetery were shrouded with ice and frost and appeared like hunched figures shivering in the night. But beneath a blanket of snow, the sharp points of the glass flower bouquet her family made had pricked the mist. The bouquet had been a great success, and soon the Wickhams had been asked by the wealthier villagers to create others for their relatives who were buried in the cemetery. But Bess knew that beneath the snow there were still the real violets she'd planted almost a year ago, now muffled in their winter sleep, ready to bloom again in spring.

"Come spring," she whispered. It was strange, but on this bitter cold night, she was not cold at all but felt insulated in some odd way. She brushed her bare hand over the sharp points of the glass bouquet. It seemed wrong. All so wrong. She wanted to smash it.

Then do! a voice swirled out of the mist.

"Grannie?" she whispered. On this frosty night, she felt something melt inside her. A joy spread throughout her.

Yes, smash them!

Not with her hand—she would bleed. She thought for a moment. Her shoe, her boot. She stood up and stomped on the flowers, then stomped again. There was a satisfying crackling, then a crunch, as she ground the heel of her boot into the snow. Crystals scattered about. Not simply crystals from the crushed bouquet, but cristallos beneath it. Her eyes opened wide with wonder.

"My daich?" she whispered. "This is my daich!" Although she was not yet sixteen, she knew this was true. Then she gasped as she realized they were not like any crystals of any daich she had ever seen. They were black, as if countless black mirrors had been smashed.

Fear not, said the voice of her grandmother. *Now watch carefully, my dear.*

The black crystals had settled into a neat little pile, then swirled up in a soft breeze.

Watch! the voice commanded.

The whirlwind of crystals soon expanded into a whirlpool. She shut her eyes, fearful that the slivers of glass might cut her.

Open your eyes, dear girl. Open them; there is nothing to fear.

Bess opened her eyes. The mist and fog had lifted. She

felt something in her hand. It was long, perhaps the length of her arm from her elbow to her wrist. It seemed to sparkle with dewdrops and ice crystals. It was not black at all but translucent as ice, yet warm in her hand.

"What in the world?" she whispered to herself.

What in the world? The wand, your wand, dear Bess.

"Is this what Mamma was looking for under my bed?"

Most likely.

"But what am I to do with it?"

I can't tell you. That is for you to learn. But look for the door.

"The door? What door?" Bess asked.

The door . . . in the ancient . . . But the voice was fading.

The mist was now engulfing the graveyard. The world suddenly seemed hollow to Bess. She felt a nothingness enveloping her, until Ulli's bright face melted out of the emptiness of this strange night and the owl alighted on her shoulder. She still clutched the wand in her hand.

"A wand, Ulli. A magic wand. But I don't know how to get the magic out of it."

"Maybe the magic is in you."

"That doesn't make sense. Then why would I need a wand?"

"Maybe you need each other to work?"

That still didn't make sense to Bess, but she was feeling cold now.

"Guide me back, Ulli. Back to the cave."

11

CHIMES IN THE MISTS

As Bess and Ulli left the graveyard, the mists of that night became thicker, almost impenetrable. They had walked for perhaps an hour or more. A slight breeze began to blow, and with it came the sound of chimes.

"We're not near any church, are we, Ulli?"

"No."

"If I am to find a door, Ulli, I certainly don't know how I'll ever see it unless I bump into it. Hupp!" she exclaimed, and fell to the ground. "I guess I just did," she said, laughing. "Ulli, where are you?"

"Right up here."

Bess tipped her head up. "On the door-frame?"

"Yes, but . . . there are no walls. How can you have a door, and a doorway, with no walls?" But there had already been so many impossible things on this night.

As if Bess were testing the coldness of water before plunging into a pond, she carefully dipped one foot over the threshold of the door and then stepped over the remains of what had been the threshold. She immediately felt something different, something otherworldly, as if she had entered a new universe—magical, obscure, and yet safe.

I am protected here, she thought.

"These trees!" Ulli gasped.

"I have never seen such enormous trees in all my life. They must be very old." Bess caught her breath. "ANCIENT!" Her grannie's last word now tolled loudly in her brain. "That's what Grannie said, her last word to me—*ancient*." And then she whispered another word. "Aosmhor."

"What?" Ulli asked, perching on her shoulder.

"This is the forest of Aosmhor." She paused. "*Aosmhor* means *ancient* in the old language of druids . . ."

"It's . . . it's not *glaumora*, is it?"

"What's glaumora?"

"The owl word for *heaven*. If it is, then we're dead."

Bess smiled and looked at her shoulder. A fringe feather of Ulli's was about to drop. She reached up and plucked it.

"Ouch!" Ulli exclaimed.

"See, you're not dead!" Bess giggled.

The mists had cleared. Bess stood in several inches of snow and looked up. The tops of these trees pricked at the sky. "*Crann lubhair*," she whispered.

"What?" Ulli asked.

"Yew trees. Maybe the oldest trees in the world. Thousands upon thousands of years. Life and death trees. Grannie once told me. Their red berries are poisonous. But down here, poking through the snow, is a yew shoot." She tipped her head up toward Ulli. The under feathers of his wings were pure white. The owl appeared now like a pale angel over her head. "We are in a strange place, Ulli."

They saw there were other ancient trees, cedars that might have been older than yews. The snow kept falling. The moon rose and bleached the snow even whiter. The girl's and the owl's shadows stretched longer into the night, as if feeling their way toward some unknown destination in this ancient forest. The only sounds now were the chimes, which had grown dimmer, the wind wrapping around them, and the squeak of Bess's boots in the snow. She remembered something her grannie once said: *It is in the dark that eyes begin to see.* And it was in the darkest of the dark that Bess first spied what might be her home: an ancient oak that towered over the forest.

She tipped her head up toward Ulli.

"We're home, Ulli. We're home."

Bess immediately began climbing the tree. She would

have climbed to the moon if she had to. But halfway up, she found a pocket where three massive limbs flowed together and formed a moss-lined hammock. Clutching the wand, she curled up and fell into a deep, dreamless sleep. Ulli perched above her and spread his wings to protect her against the snow that had begun to fall. In that one-thousand-year-old tree, it might have seemed to an ordinary human that this girl and the owl were from a distant galaxy.

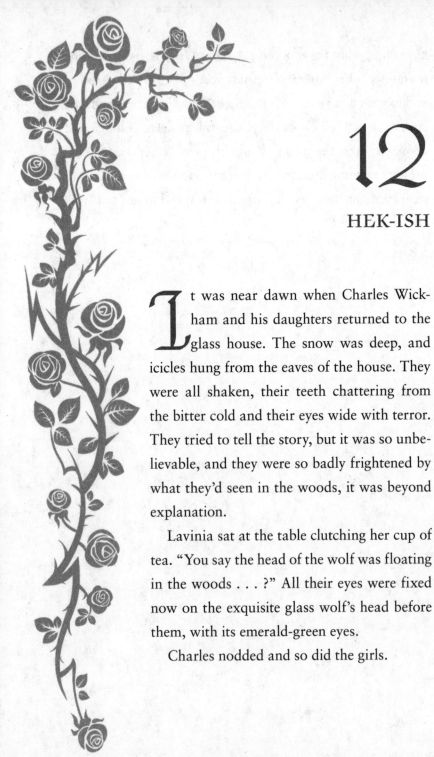

12

HEK-ISH

It was near dawn when Charles Wickham and his daughters returned to the glass house. The snow was deep, and icicles hung from the eaves of the house. They were all shaken, their teeth chattering from the bitter cold and their eyes wide with terror. They tried to tell the story, but it was so unbelievable, and they were so badly frightened by what they'd seen in the woods, it was beyond explanation.

Lavinia sat at the table clutching her cup of tea. "You say the head of the wolf was floating in the woods . . . ?" All their eyes were fixed now on the exquisite glass wolf's head before them, with its emerald-green eyes.

Charles nodded and so did the girls.

"You mean the wolf's soul escaped the glass?" Lavinia asked in a shaky voice.

"So it would seem," Charles muttered. He could not bear to look at the glass head a second longer and turned away.

"But that is impossible, Charles."

"Mamma," Olivia said. "Have you looked everywhere for Grannie's wand?"

"I've told you time and again. Everywhere. It's nowhere."

"And when did you last see it?" Rose asked.

"I told you. On our wedding day. Grannie drew the sun around us for good luck and happiness. She held up the wand and made a circle over our heads in the direction of the sun. It was somewhat embarrassing having all these old druid rituals when there haven't been any druids in nearly a thousand years. I know Pastor Filkins was simply mortified. Only heathens do these old druid things. I remember your father saying that the next thing Grannie would be doing was dancing naked through the village on the night of the full moon."

"Grannie did that?" Rose gasped.

"No, never."

"But what about Bess?"

"What about her?" their mother asked.

"Would Bess dance naked in the full moon?"

"How could you say such a thing?"

"Bess was strange, Mamma, and now she's gone. Just

disappeared. Where do you think she has gone?" Rose said. The girls exchanged a look.

"Remember, Mamma, when you saw her sprinkling salt on the back doorstep? She said it was to keep the beetles away from the marigolds. But Nanny Cobb in the village says salt can draw witches."

Their mother put her hand to her mouth. "Oh dear, I forgot that."

"She seemed like such a simple child, you know. Never took to the family craft, though . . ." Charles said.

"But the druid blood runs weak in our family." Lavinia sighed deeply. "If it had been the Holmans or even the Fitz-gibbonses I'd understand. But why would Bess run away? I don't think she ever actually saw one of our animal extractions." She paused for several seconds. "Unless she somehow spied on us."

"No, we were always careful," Charles Wickham said. "And that reminds me."

"Reminds you of what?" Lavinia looked up at her husband.

"When I first found the bags of the dark crystals from which I made the black mirrors, there were four bags. We've used two. But now there is only one."

"How could that be?" Rose asked. "Are you sure, Papa?"

"Absolutely. Well, at least we have enough for now. And I'm going to experiment with reusing the shattered black mirrors."

"Charles," Lavinia said. "Remember that rainstorm the other day? There was a bit of flooding in the cellar. You don't suppose it could have gotten to the bags—were the cristallos swept away?"

"Bag and all?" her husband asked.

"What about the bag with Bess's daich?" Olivia asked.

"It's still . . . untouched," Charles Wickham said.

"I wonder if she'll come back for it when she turns sixteen?" Lavinia mused.

"Maybe not, Mamma," Olivia said.

"Yes," Charles said. "And perhaps that would be for the best."

Lavinia's brow crinkled. "With Bess gone and winter upon us, the garden is hardly thriving. If she doesn't come back by spring, we'll need more help in the garden to attract animals. We might have to hire a char girl."

"Yes, no fancy thoughts with a char girl," Rose said.

Olivia nodded. "You know Bess did have these very fancy, strange ideas."

Their father sighed deeply. "But there was always something hek-ish about the child." He touched his heart as he said the dangerous word—as he did any word to do with witches or witchish things. It was an ancient custom to touch one's heart when one said a forbidden or dangerous word like *hek-ish*.

That night, all four of the Wickhams fell into a troubled sleep. As a blade of moonlight dropped through the window across the bed that Charles Wickham and his wife slept in, Charles saw the wolf's head in his dreams. The emerald eyes blazed through the darkness of his sleep. And then his daughter Bess's eyes, also green, seemed to flash through his mind.

"Hek-ish, by God!" He sat up straight in a cold sweat. Climbing out of bed, he went to the hot shop and took the wolf's head from the shelf above the cooling oven. Picking it up, he smashed it. Shattered crystals spread across the floor, glittering darkly in the night.

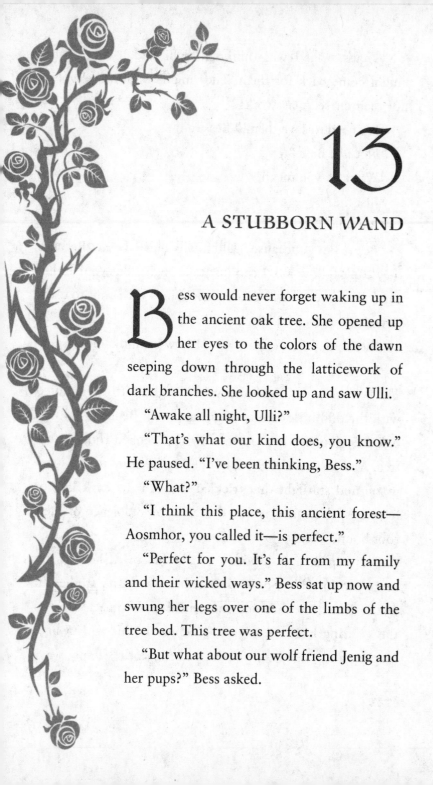

13

A STUBBORN WAND

Bess would never forget waking up in the ancient oak tree. She opened up her eyes to the colors of the dawn seeping down through the latticework of dark branches. She looked up and saw Ulli.

"Awake all night, Ulli?"

"That's what our kind does, you know." He paused. "I've been thinking, Bess."

"What?"

"I think this place, this ancient forest—Aosmhor, you called it—is perfect."

"Perfect for you. It's far from my family and their wicked ways." Bess sat up now and swung her legs over one of the limbs of the tree bed. This tree was perfect.

"But what about our wolf friend Jenig and her pups?" Bess asked.

"That's what I was thinking," Ulli said. "Your family might come back for them. They might want more wolves for their cursed glassworks."

"We need to save them!" Bess said.

"Not *we*, Bess."

"What do you mean?"

"Just me."

"But why?"

"Be . . . be . . . because," Ulli finally blurted out. "Because they can't follow me. I can just take flight. But your father can follow you. And he could bring others with guns to track down the wolves." Deep in Ulli's brain was the shadow of another thought, one that was for now unthinkable.

The wolves soon came and were delighted to be reunited with the odd little family of girl and owl. Beneath the vast oak they found a cave formed by the webbed roots of the tree. And as Bess delighted in opening her eyes to the silver moon and starlight that trickled through the dark lace of branches, the wolves enjoyed the earthy redolence of their root-bound shelter.

Bess herself had decided to make her own shelter a bit more comfortable. She looked at her wand and studied it. She reflected on that odd moment it had come to her, in the swirling bits of the glass bouquet. If this truly was a magic wand, then how did she make it work? Simply wave it? There was an old druid incantation that meant, *I will create as I speak*, but she could not remember it exactly—*mi mar a labhras mi*? Now, why did that sound familiar to her? She tried for the next several days to recall the words of that old charm she had heard about.

She retraced her route back to the door she had found on that fateful night that she had heard her grannie.

Bess's first find was a narrow board as long as her arm, which must have been a windowsill. She continued scrounging around and found several bricks that must have been from a fireplace, and she soon discovered several old wooden planks. She examined one or two of them. "These might do," she whispered to herself. Her best find, however, was some roof shingles. Not that she wanted a roof exactly, as she would now always want to be able to wake up to the sky and sleep under the stars. But what if she could design or make a detachable roof? One to use only in bad weather? She looked at the wand, which she carried most of the time but was still stumped on how to use. Was it useful at all? There were little air bubbles in the glass. They sparkled like small galaxies, maybe universes. Magic universes. *How do I use you? Or . . .* She caught her breath. *Misuse you?* Was that a different voice she heard in her head? The first was her own voice, but the second? Was that Grannie? The wand grew warm in her hand. The words, the old druid words, came to her almost spontaneously.

Cruthaichidh mi mar a smaoinicheas mi agus a labhras mi.

And in that moment, she pictured what her house might look like in the old oak tree. Instincts came to her. She peered down at a wedge-shaped stone. "That could be a hammer," she whispered to herself. She looked for a good sturdy stick and soon found the perfect one, with a fork at one end. A precise vision came to her for the design of this hammer. She sat on the ground, untied her bootlace, and with it fastened the stone wedge into the fork of the stick.

She studied the wand again. It was becoming clearer to her by the second. This was not quick magic. *Trick magic*, as Grannie used to call it. The kind that hucksters plied at country fairs. No, this was true magic, real magic—magic that had to be worked at. And required Bess to think hard.

She then stood up. Even though she had removed her bootlace, her boot still felt tight. She looked down and emitted a small gasp. There was a new shoelace in her boot! This was a strange kind of magic indeed. One had to think something, figure it out, before the magic worked. One could not just wave a wand around and babble some spell. She looked at the wand. It was cool again. If she was going to build a house, she was first going to have to think it.

She spent the rest of the day collecting scraps. The wolves and Ulli joined her in transporting all the pieces that would eventually become her house.

"All roof shingles over there." She pointed with the wand.

"Boards like this." She held up a broad plank. "These will

be floorboards. Over there"—she pointed to a stump—"put the wall planks and the ledges for windowsills."

"And glass for the windows?" Ulli asked.

"No glass!"

"B-b-but," Ulli stammered.

"My house will not have windows of glass. And no door. A house in a tree needs no door. At least not a proper door. The trunk is its doorway."

"An improper door," yelped one of the pups.

"Exactly. An improper door in an improper house. But I promise you it shall be the loveliest of all houses." She looked down again at the wand and thought, *With this stubborn wand I shall build my improper house!*

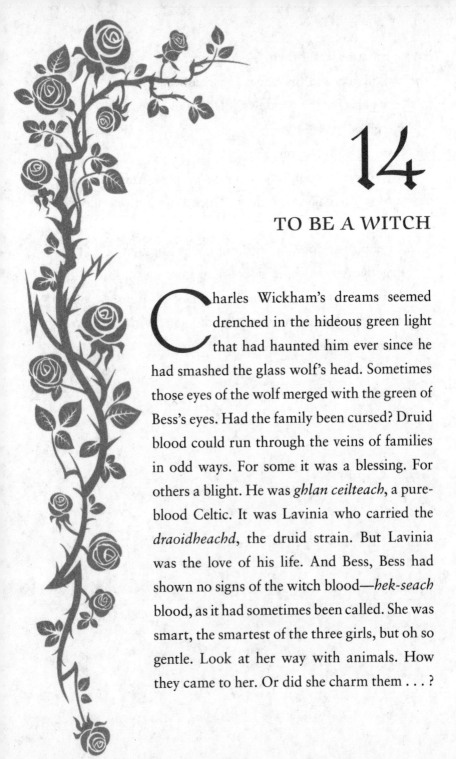

14

TO BE A WITCH

Charles Wickham's dreams seemed drenched in the hideous green light that had haunted him ever since he had smashed the glass wolf's head. Sometimes those eyes of the wolf merged with the green of Bess's eyes. Had the family been cursed? Druid blood could run through the veins of families in odd ways. For some it was a blessing. For others a blight. He was *ghlan ceilteach*, a pure-blood Celtic. It was Lavinia who carried the *draoidheachd*, the druid strain. But Lavinia was the love of his life. And Bess, Bess had shown no signs of the witch blood—*hek-seach* blood, as it had sometimes been called. She was smart, the smartest of the three girls, but oh so gentle. Look at her way with animals. How they came to her. Or did she charm them . . . ?

Perhaps cast an enchantment on those animals? Had she in fact cast an enchantment on all of them? He began to shake uncontrollably. He got out of bed and went to the kitchen, where Lavinia was stirring the porridge.

"Stop!" he hissed.

Lavinia wheeled about with the porridge spoon still in her hand, dripping on the rim of the pot.

"Charles! What is it? You look like you've seen a ghost."

"It's your daughter." He inhaled deeply.

"My daughter?"

"Yes, your daughter Bess." Tears sprang to his eyes. "I fear she is a witch."

"Bess, a witch? But how is that possible?"

"It must be your mother."

"Grannie? Grannie was a witch?"

"Possibly," Charles replied. He could not meet her eyes.

"B-b-b-but . . . but they say it only happens once in a century. There was thought to be one before Grannie, and that was maybe forty years ago. And if Grannie was one . . . No, no, it would be too soon."

"It's happened. I'm sure. The wolf, it had green eyes just like Bess's, like Grannie's. She is ungodly. A witch for sure."

Olivia had tiptoed down the stairs and was crouched behind the kitchen door, listening. Her eyes were wide with a terrifying glare of delight mixed with horror, or perhaps it was vengeance. *Wait until I tell Rose . . . but not now*, she counseled herself. *Be patient.*

Later that morning, Olivia sneaked into the kitchen. Her parents were busy in the hot shop preparing a titmouse, a charming small bird that they had fed the melted crystal. The suffering bird was now staggering around in the small cage lined with mirrors, becoming completely addled.

She knew that in the table's utensil drawer there were a few old very tarnished forks that her mother never used. They had only three tines, and such a fork was sometimes considered a tool of the devil. To use them meant to invite temptation and evil into a house, but to just throw them away could also cause evil across the land. They were wrapped in a black cloth with cinders from hearth fires, thought to contain their vileness.

Carefully, Olivia drew a fork from the black cloth. She tiptoed upstairs and went to the room where the three sisters had slept. Lifting the mattress of the bed where Bess had once slept, she tucked the fork under it. She then coughed and began to unmake the bed.

"What are you doing, Olivia?" Rose said sleepily.

"I thought since Bess isn't here, we could use her blankets. It will be getting colder. Why not use these?" At just that moment, there was a clinking sound.

"What's that?" Rose asked.

"Hmmm . . . something dropped on the floor."

Rose was out of bed and on her knees. She emitted a little screech.

"What is it?"

Rose backed out from under the bed. Her face was pale. "There's a fork under there, Olivia . . . a three-tined fork."

The girls ran down the stairs and burst into the hot shop.

"Not now, girls, not now!" their mother warned. "We are at a delicate moment here. This stupid titmouse has proven quite a little devil, he has."

The girls glanced at the shattered mirrors and the torn-up body of the titmouse. With one wing askew, the other was caught in a strange wild flight of its own, with no body attached. A glistening vaporous cloud began to form in the mirrored box over the remnant body parts of the titmouse.

"There it comes!" their mamma said with a rapturous voice. "Its soul!"

A few seconds later, their mother turned to them.

"Now, what is it, girls?"

"Under Bess's mattress," Rose said. "A fork."

"A three-tined fork," Olivia added. Lavinia went white and turned to Charles. "So, husband, you were right."

Plough Monday, the first Monday after Twelfth Night, fell on the ninth of January. The Wickhams were bundled into their four-in-hand, a serviceable vehicle that could carry three in the cab and two in the driver's seat. They had hitched up their two sturdy ponies and headed off to Cockle's Mount, the largest town in Crop Shire County, where the magistrates' offices were located.

"Oh dear," Lavinia moaned. "I forgot about this being a market town on Plough Monday. Just look at all these men with their ploughs; they're all clogging the way."

"Look, Mamma, in the churchyard!" Rose exclaimed.

"Ah, the long sword dance!" Charles Wickham laughed. "Used to join in when I was a boy."

"Oh my, someone is approaching with a hag."

"I see the old lady, Mamma, but what is that other thing . . . ?"

"A fool dressed as some sort of animal." Then the creature danced up to their four-in-hand.

"A penny for your thoughts, driver."

Charles Wickham looked at the man, who wore a wolf's head. Then his own heart seemed to stop, for the eyes that looked back at him were blazing green. "Aargh!" Charles gasped and yowled. The horses reared and charged. People scattered as the horses galloped down the street. Lavinia reached over and grabbed the reins.

"I've got them . . . I've got them, Charles." And quickly she brought them under her control just in front of the magistrates' court. She turned to her husband. "Whatever happened to you, my dear?"

Charles swallowed. "Erm . . . it . . . it was . . . that creature who danced up to us . . . so . . . so like . . ."

"The wolf?"

"Yes." Charles slumped a bit. "I fear, my dear, that a . . .

a . . ." He began to speak and then crossed his fingers oddly.

"Don't, Charles! Don't!" Lavinia grabbed her husband's hand and untangled his index and middle finger. "That's just country nonsense—you know that, Charles. We're here now. The magistrates will hear our case and resolve the situation." She now turned to Olivia. "You have the evidence ready?" Olivia sat clutching the cast-iron box that held the fork and nodded. "You brought the sprig of heart wort?"

"In the box, Mamma."

"Good. They say it's the best protection from the tines of the fork."

The family entered the hulking building. After being directed through numerous corridors sliced by ominous shadows, they took their seats on a bench to wait to see the magistrates. After an hour's wait, they were ushered into the courtroom. Behind a high bench, three bewhiskered men sat. One gaunt, another rather plumpish with a face reddened by drink, the other a young man whose gracious countenance was spoiled by a thin-lipped sliver of a mouth that had likely never smiled.

The thin-lipped man turned toward a young fellow. "The clerk's papers, please." He quickly reviewed the papers, along with the letter that Charles had written.

Several minutes passed as the three magistrates reviewed the papers. They tipped their heads together as they huddled to speak in low whispers.

"Might the evidence be brought forth?"

Charles stood up. "Yes, Honorable Curtwell. Our daughter Olivia found the three-tined fork under the mattress of our lost daughter, Bess."

"Step forward, Mistress Wickham."

Olivia stepped forward. She flushed. Her hands trembled as she clutched the metal box with the fork. She was frightened and yet pleased. Every single eye in the courtroom was upon her. She stood up straighter, a bold and proud look in her eyes.

"And, Mistress Wickham, have you taken proper precautions in transporting the item of concern?"

"Yes, Honorable Curtwell. I have put a sprig of heart wort in the box."

"Excellent, my dear."

At this, Lavinia gave Charles's hand a squeeze. Next, the magistrate in the middle asked that Olivia retell how she came upon the fork. She told the story, explaining that her sister had run away perhaps a month or more before.

"And why had she left home?"

"I . . . I'm not sure."

"She had never taken to glassmaking, like my other daughters," Charles Wickham interrupted.

"Please, sir," the questioning magistrate cut him off. "You shall have your turn."

And Charles Wickham did have his turn, and so did his wife, and so did Rose. They painted a most dire picture for the three magistrates.

"Do you feel, Mrs. Wickham, that this was some sort of lure from the devil himself?"

"Well, I suppose so. How else would she have . . ."

"Found it?" the thin-lipped magistrate asked.

Olivia looked down into her lap, where she twisted a handkerchief.

"Exactly!" Lavinia replied. But, of course, she knew how it had been found. Years before, Grannie had brought them into the house and Lavinia had shoved them into the very back of the kitchen drawer, wrapped in black cloth with cinders, as Grannie had instructed her. It was before any of her three daughters had been born. So long ago that she had forgotten.

The magistrates then excused themselves to a small room off the main one to deliberate.

Fifteen minutes later, they returned and resumed their places behind the high desk. The small, plump man in the middle slammed down his gavel twice. "By order of the magistrates of Crop Shire County, we hereby issue a warrant of arrest for Bess Wickham for suspected witchcraft."

It started to snow lightly as the family made their way home. They were quiet, each alone with their own thoughts. Olivia's jaw jutted with determination—she knew how right she was about Bess. She was proud that she had testified in front of the magistrates. Proud of how they had believed her and now had issued a warrant for Bess's arrest. For Olivia, the story of the fork beneath the mattress was becoming more real every second. The trip she had made to the kitchen at dawn was blurring in her memory. But the image of the fork beneath the mattress burned brightly. She rationalized in her own mind that Bess had known about the fork all along but had not brought it up to the bedroom the girls shared for fear her sisters might discover it. She had soon convinced herself that she had often heard the creak of the stairs as Bess descended to the kitchen at odd hours of the night for these rendezvous with the devil. Rose thought how lucky it was that Olivia had found the cursed object. She wondered how they had ever survived having such a sister without her doing real harm to all of them.

Their mother's voice broke the silence. "You know, Charles, the child . . . She was born with a caul on her head."

"You mean, the birth sac was around her head?"

"Yes," she said softly.

"But that is supposed to be good, bring luck. It means a gifted child."

"Yes, so they say. But the problem was, it was only half of the birth sac, which can mean cursed. Grannie removed it and she told me not to worry. But there is a particular way one must bury the sac, and I'm not sure Grannie did it right." She sighed. "You know how she had her old druid ways about things." She sniffled a bit, then turned to her husband. "Charles"—a sob tore from her throat—"I have fouled my family with this blood."

"Nonsense, Lavinia. That blood only runs in the veins of one of our children. Just one—Bess." He inhaled deeply. "And when she is caught, well, that will be the end of it."

"You don't blame me, do you?"

"Of course not." Charles sighed. Lavinia glanced at him. His jaw was set. "It's the devil's work. The devil and Grannie. And you know, Grannie had green eyes, and so does Bess. But not you or Olivia or Rose. All pale gray, like mine. There is strangeness with that child. Believe me, wife."

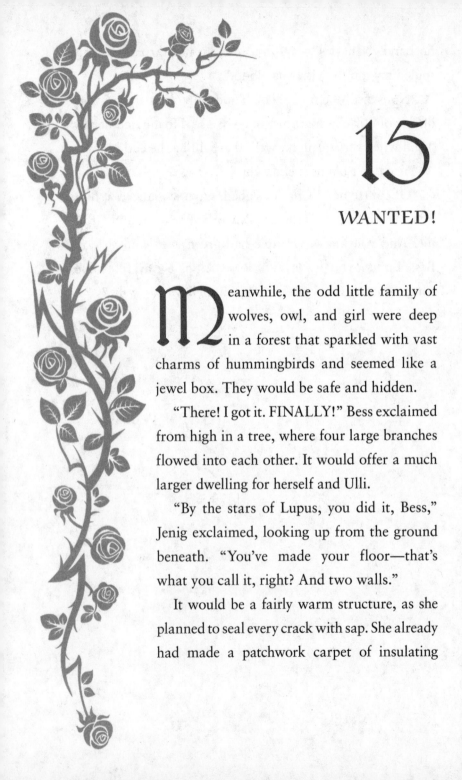

15

WANTED!

Meanwhile, the odd little family of wolves, owl, and girl were deep in a forest that sparkled with vast charms of hummingbirds and seemed like a jewel box. They would be safe and hidden.

"There! I got it. FINALLY!" Bess exclaimed from high in a tree, where four large branches flowed into each other. It would offer a much larger dwelling for herself and Ulli.

"By the stars of Lupus, you did it, Bess," Jenig exclaimed, looking up from the ground beneath. "You've made your floor—that's what you call it, right? And two walls."

It would be a fairly warm structure, as she planned to seal every crack with sap. She already had made a patchwork carpet of insulating moss. To do this, she had collected every shade of green in the spectrum of moss—some bright green, others grayish green, and a rare species of blue moss. She was so entranced with the beauty of her carpet that she decided to make herself a cloak of moss sewn together by spider silk. Her skills with the wand were improving daily. It wasn't as easy as it might appear. She had to think hard, then draw a picture in her mind's eye, a plan of sorts. It was not simply blathering nonsensical words like *abracadabra*, or just humming an incantation or a perky little tune, then waving the wand about. No, there was quite a bit more to invoking magic. There were no shortcuts. It took rigor, discipline, concentration, and imagination.

She looked down to where the wolf was standing on the ground and gave the wand a little kiss. "Everyone thinks that with a magic wand it's all so easy. Well, it's not. One just can't mumble *abracadabra* and all that nonsense."

It had taken Bess months to learn about the wand. And she was not yet an expert by any means. Food and clothing were easily mastered once she got the basics. But Bess was determined to make a tree house—not just a tree house but one that connected with Ulli's hollow—and that required months of concentration and practice with the wand. Ulli considered ground living simply unnatural for an owl, uncivilized. He believed that ground living dulled an owl's greatest attributes—sense of hearing, sense of smell—and made for weak primary feathers.

Bess's reasons were simpler. She felt safer in a tree. She could see anyone approaching. And above all, she loved what she called the music of a tree. The sounds of the wind stirring in its branches, the fluttering of leaves, and in an elder tree, the soft complaints as they creaked or moaned. Yes, she even found a kind of solace in those sounds. It made for a bond between them in almost the same way that she remembered when she used to rub her grannie's feet with liniment or massage her arthritic hands. Now she had created a floor, and she was moving on to the walls and the furnishings. She wanted a proper tree house with a bed for sleeping and a table for writing. Although Ulli had brought her many things, Bess had learned how to use the wand to create some of the basics that she needed.

Ulli was off today on a flight that would take him to the village of Wee-on-the-Way, which was close—too close, Bess felt—to the glass house. But Ulli often found things near the village that people had cast off. Ink for the quills that Ulli happily gave her when he shed them, scraps of cloth, paper for drawing, stockings blown from a clothesline, even candles, although Bess did not yet know how to create a small flame with her magic wand.

"Don't worry about me, Bess," Ulli said. "Trust me. I'm not going anywhere near the glass house. But I have a longing for trout, and the best trout streams are right near Way River . . ."

Bess settled down for the night, her first night in her almost house. She had a floor. She had bedding. And as she looked up through the lace of the branches, the stars sparkled like a net of jewels. *What more does a person need?* she thought. She tucked the wand close to her chest and drifted off into a deep sleep.

At the same time, the barn owl was sweeping down across the town square of Wee-on-the-Way. With a belly full of trout and one in his talons, Ulli liked to explore the windows of the fine crystal shop. Were the Wickhams still up to their evil and despicable practices? The owners of this shop, the MacGivors, had bought many of those dreadful figurines from the Wickhams' dreadful ovens. What new animals' souls had been sucked from their beings? Ulli was surprised that the wolf's head had not been given a second "life." That, after all, was what had driven Bess to the forest. But it had never appeared in the shop window.

At this hour of the night, there was not a soul on the narrow, twisting street of the crystal shop. Ulli alighted right on the windowsill. The figurines in the window were the same: A very small fawn that had been lured by the raspberry patch that Bess had planted and that she now cursed. Several rabbits and five hummingbirds. No wolf's head. There was a sign in the window with the royal seal, designating that the goods of this store supplied products and services to the queen.

Crystal World of Animals
Created exclusively for our shop
By appointment to HM the Queen

But when Ulli turned toward the lamppost, he caught sight of a poster that shocked him to his wing bones. "Harrumph," Ulli gurgled in disgust, and gasped. His beak opened in dismay. The fish dropped to the cobblestones as he lifted himself from the window. He hovered in flight in front of the notice on the post, gasping when he saw a face he certainly recognized beneath the large letters:

WANTED!
Bess Wickham
For Use of the Devil's Magic—Witchcraft
Beware—May Be Dangerous
Reward for Her Capture!

It was Bess's face! With his heart beating wildly and his gizzard clenched in fear, Ulli ripped the notice from the post. Unthinkable! He flew off and blessed the sturdy wind that would boost his speed back to Bess.

When Ulli reached the hidden woods, he caught sight of Bess's slender figure on a branch outside the half-built dwelling high up in the tree. Bess was balanced somewhat precariously on one limb. "I'm just practicing with the wand,

Ulli. I think we need to add on a room, a study or library, or maybe even a nursery for abandoned baby creatures or wounded ones." She glanced at the owl. "Now what have you got, Ulli?"

"You're not going to like it."

"Really, now?" Her eyes opened wide. "Well, set yourself down." She tucked the wand under her arm.

It was a wonder what Bess had done to this dwelling. For furnishings, Ulli himself had picked up assorted bric-a-brac. There was not room for chairs, but there were other small accessories, like plates and cups. But no glass! Never glass. Cups were made from hollowed-out burls, the rounded knots that grew on many trees. Eating utensils, which Ulli considered ridiculous—even for beakless creatures—might be anything from a small, forked branch or piece of wood, and a spoon could be an empty chestnut. With a small modification from the wand, a handle could be attached. They lived in a kind of natural splendor of domesticity, where lichen became lace tablecloths and autumn leaves were turned into rich tapestries with the proper touch of the wand.

"So, what have we here?" Bess asked.

Ulli began to unroll the wanted poster.

Constabulary of WEE-ON-THE-WAY: Young female Bess Wickham wanted for theft and suspected witchcraft. 110 pounds, 5 feet 2 inches, red hair, some spots.

Bess's eyes widened in horror. "Wh-wh-what!" she began to stammer. How had this happened? Had they turned on her? Her own family?

"Witchcraft! Theft! Spots!" She took a deep breath. "I don't have spots!"

"I . . . I think they mean freckles." Ulli hooted softly.

"No! This has Olivia written all over it. She has spots. Spots are different from freckles. You squeeze them and they pop, and goo comes out. See this? This is a freckle." Bess touched the bridge of her nose. "And witchcraft . . . ? They are the ones who steal souls! Someday, if I get better with this wand, I'll *save* souls. Every single one of those hummingbirds, those rabbits, the baby squirrels, the barn kittens, the souls they ripped out of every woodland creature for their precious figurines, I'll get them back. And it's not going to be by any witchcraft."

"If not witchcraft, then what? What's it going to be?" Ulli asked.

Bess closed her eyes. "Grannie craft. That's what it is." She picked up the wand and stared at it for the longest time before she spoke. "Or . . . or . . . maybe it's fae craft."

"Fae? What's fae?"

"Fairy craft. Ulli, I might be only fourteen, but in my heart, I think I am very old. Not so old as to be a grannie." She paused and took a deep breath. "But old enough to be a fairy godmother, perhaps," Bess whispered, and looked off into some liminal space that was neither here nor there, but some invisible threshold in time. "Yes, a *bandia*."

"What?" Ulli's beak dropped open.

"A fairy godmother. That is what it was called in the old Celtic language—a bandia."

Part Three

GREENWICH

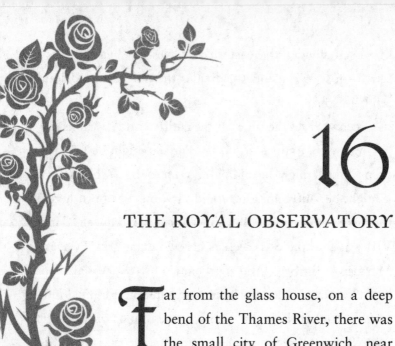

16

THE ROYAL OBSERVATORY

F ar from the glass house, on a deep bend of the Thames River, there was the small city of Greenwich, near London, where some say time was invented. Not really, of course, but it was indeed as if a grand and invisible earth clock had been set there. The invisible clock had a name—Greenwich Mean Time. Greenwich was located at the prime meridian of the world, at longitude zero degrees, zero minutes, zero seconds. Triple zero! Although the line was imaginary, there was in fact an actual symbolic line that scored the courtyard of the observatory, indicating the beginning of the prime meridian.

Every place on Earth is measured in terms of its distance east or west from this line. The line itself divides the eastern and western hemispheres of Earth—just as the equator divides the northern and southern hemispheres.

Greenwich set the time for the entire world. If it was noon in Greenwich, to the east, in, say, Paris, it might be 1:00 p.m., or in China it might be midnight, or far to the west in America it might be 7:00 a.m. One could say time was born here, in the town of Greenwich. But so were kings and queens. Henry VIII was born here, as well as his two daughters, Princesses Mary and Elizabeth. And a girl named Estrella was also born here. She was neither a princess nor a queen, nor any kind of royalty. Nonetheless, she lived on the grounds of the Greenwich Royal Observatory. Her grandfather was an official keeper of the lenses of the Merz Great Equatorial Telescope, in the Meridian Building of the Royal Observatory.

Estrella now stood with one foot in either hemisphere, with each foot planted on either side of the groove in the pavement that marked the meridian line. On the west side of the line, the word *Dublin* was engraved, with its longitude indicating it was six degrees and fifteen minutes from Greenwich. On the east side of the line was the word *Berlin*, indicating it was thirteen degrees and twenty-five minutes to the east of Greenwich. *A foot in two worlds*, she thought, *and yet I am nowhere.*

"Come along, dearie, or you'll be late for your granddad's funeral."

Estrella continued walking toward the chapel. But after that, where would she go? She had no one. Her parents had died long ago, and ever since she could remember she had been cared for by her grandfather. But now he was gone, and the house they had lived in was owned by the Royal Observatory. It would be given to the new lens keeper. For that was what her grandfather, Barnaby Diggerton, had done—ground the lenses for the great Merz telescope. The largest so far that century. In his role as lens keeper, he also made all the necessary adjustments to maintain the telescope. All the lenses needed to be cleaned several times a month. Dirt on a lens could scatter light and make dark skies less dark and bright objects less crisp. All screws, nuts, and bolts needed to be oiled so that all parts of the scope moved smoothly—smooth as silk, as her grandfather would say. The columns of the scope had to be perfectly aligned and their alignment checked every day for accuracy.

"Come along, child," Mrs. Welles, the housekeeper, urged. She took Estrella by the elbow. "Look, a nice turnout for your granddad." She raised her hand and shaded her eyes from the sun. "Half a dozen *Obs*, at least. I see Sir Morton over there. You know his daughter Eloise, don't you?"

"Not really," Estrella murmured.

"Oh, now, why not? Such a lovely girl."

Not really, Estrella thought. And Mrs. Welles knew perfectly well why not.

Within this community, there were social stratifications of which the children were keenly aware, perhaps more so than the adults. But for a child, the highest level one's father could achieve was to be in the "Obs," an astronomer working with the big telescope. Next there were the "Clocks." These men were mathematicians who did all the calculations pertaining to movement of the stars across the sky, as well as compiling the lunar and astral tables of the sun and the moons and the planets, used by sailors. Finally, there were the "Relics." The Relics were the curators of the museum and the people like Estrella's grandfather who were the caretakers of all the delicate tools and equipment that the astronomers used to do their calculations and observations of astral bodies and celestial events. These differences in social stations were felt most acutely among the children of Greenwich. The arrogant Obs children tended to be gossips or snitches and excruciatingly snooty. The children of Clocks were bullies and lickspittles, always sucking up to the Obs.

Now she caught sight of Daphne and her mother, Adelia. Daphne's father was a Relic. But as the mother and daughter approached to offer their condolences, there seemed to be something different about them.

"Our condolences, dear child," Adelia said. She was extremely well-dressed for this service. Although appropriate for a funeral, Estrella could see that her gown must have been made by the finest dressmaker in Greenwich, Madame

La Rue. Daphne herself was wearing an extremely elegant dress. She gave a weak little smile to Estrella and smoothed the bodice, which was heavily embroidered in a dark stitching suitable for a funeral. Although she uttered no words, Daphne seemed to be calling attention to her dress, as if to say, *Look at me in my splendid Madame La Rue mourning gown.*

"W-w-w-w-would you like to sit with me, Daphne . . . and, of course, your mamma, too?"

Daphne's expression froze. "Er . . . uh . . ."

"Oh, that's not possible, dear," her mother replied. "You see, my husband and I will be sitting with Sir Huggins, director of spectroscopic studies. George is a Clock now. No longer a Relic." She giggled slightly. "I guess he's outgrown that! Sir Huggins keeps him busy with the calculations, and we are sitting in his pew for the service. It seems only proper. I'm sure you understand."

In truth, Estrella did not understand at all. What she did understand was that there had been a social shift, and she and Daphne were now at far ends of the friendship spectrum. She herself at the cooling end. But Daphne and her mother and father, the Brownings—like a comet perhaps—had soared to greater heights on the social scale. In astronomical terms, one minute millions of years ago, the Brownings were just specks of junk composed of rock, ice, and dust, and the next minute they were racing closer to the sun. The family was heating up and spewing gases into a glowing head that could become as large as a planet. As large as Sir Huggins, the discoverer of the Orion nebula.

"Now where will you live, child?"

"I . . . I'm not sure."

"Your grandfather made no plans for you?"

"I . . . I don't think he expected to die." And now the next thing Estrella said shocked even her. "Comets die, you know. When they fly too close to the sun, they vaporize and turn into gas."

Mrs. Browning looked at her and tightened her grip on Daphne's hand. "Come along, my dear. I see your father ahead with Sir Huggins."

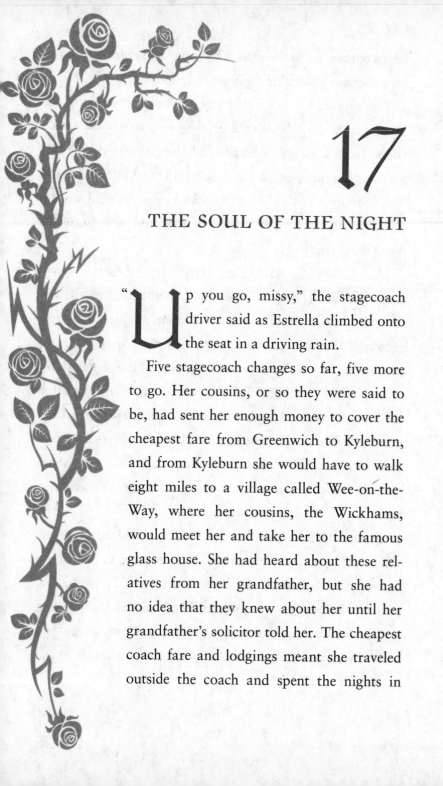

17

THE SOUL OF THE NIGHT

"Up you go, missy," the stagecoach driver said as Estrella climbed onto the seat in a driving rain.

Five stagecoach changes so far, five more to go. Her cousins, or so they were said to be, had sent her enough money to cover the cheapest fare from Greenwich to Kyleburn, and from Kyleburn she would have to walk eight miles to a village called Wee-on-the-Way, where her cousins, the Wickhams, would meet her and take her to the famous glass house. She had heard about these relatives from her grandfather, but she had no idea that they knew about her until her grandfather's solicitor told her. The cheapest coach fare and lodgings meant she traveled outside the coach and spent the nights in barns connected to the inns. The trip took several days, and now she was almost halfway there.

The rain had stopped. Luckily she had spent part of the last bit of money the Wickhams had sent to her for a new rubberized rain cape. It had rained almost every day of this journey. But now, just as they drew into the courtyard of the inn, the rain stopped. Estrella looked up and could see the sky clearing. *Finally*, she thought. It would be a beautiful night for stargazing.

She much preferred sleeping in the barns of these wayside inns than in the rooms, where you might have to share a bed with a child or an unknown woman. And she definitely preferred the soft neighs of horses to the harsh snores of people. In the inn there was no privacy, and the rooms stank of sweat and bodily odors. The scent of hay and the large airy spaces of a stable or barn were vastly superior, in her mind. As soon as she had climbed down and paid the fees to the innkeeper, she made her way to the barn. There was a nice big hay-pitching window that faced the northeast for a perfect view of the rising stars.

She had paid the innkeeper for her dinner and in return was given half a sausage and a mug of cider. She climbed to the hayloft in the barn and from her traveling satchel took out one of the two small telescopes she had brought with her. Leaning against the pitching window, she began to scan the sky. She felt a thrill run through her as she adjusted the focus on the scope, sweeping the heavens as a housekeeper with a broom might go about her household duties. She was a servant to the night in hopes of finding some treasure to share with the entire world. She wanted to be a comet hunter like the astronomer Caroline Herschel, or perhaps discover a new dusky nebula nursery with newborn stars wrapped in its vapors. Every time she fitted her eye to the ocular lens of a telescope, she thought how many secrets there were to be discovered. So many starry friends to see again in the darkness of the universe, like Orion, stumbling across the gathering darkness dragging his sword. And so tonight she scanned the heavens, what she had come to think of as the soul of the night.

A few days later, near dawn, just as the morning star of Venus was rising, Estrella walked into the village of Wee-on-the-Way. She had been given instructions in a letter from Lavinia Wickham to go to the MacGivor & Sons fine crystal shop to wait for the Wickhams to pick her up.

Mrs. MacGivor was quite welcoming and set her down at a table, serving Estrella her first real meal in ten days: a small mound of scrambled eggs, a rasher of bacon, and a hunk of coarse bread, along with some cheese.

Estrella was in the back in the kitchen when she heard the jingle of a bell announcing a customer.

"Must be the Wickhams," said Mrs. MacGivor, a plump, jolly woman. "Too early for customers."

Estrella started to get up. "Sit right there, child. Finish your breakfast."

A minute later she came back. "Here she is. Lovely girl and such a gracious way about her. Always asking to help, even after that long walk from Kyleburn."

"Well, come along, girl," Lavinia said abruptly. "We can save your feet a bit." She then turned to Mrs. MacGivor. "How much do we owe you for her food?"

Mrs. MacGivor looked slightly shocked. "Nothing, of course, Mrs. Wickham."

"We gave her money for the carriage stops on the way." She turned to Estrella. "You used all that up, I suppose?"

"Yes, ma'am, I did. At least, most of it."

Lavinia made a sound of disapproval. "Young ones nowadays."

Mrs. MacGivor blinked, as if she had somehow lost the thread of conversation.

"Well, come along now, Ella."

"Ella?" both Estrella and Mrs. MacGivor said at once.

"Her name is Estrella," Mrs. MacGivor said rather stiffly.

"We'll just call her Ella." Mr. Wickham grunted. "Easier that way."

A dark shadow passed through Mrs. MacGivor's eyes. "I suppose so," she said softly.

Charles Wickham picked up her traveling bag. "This yours?" He looked at Estrella.

"Yes, sir." He took it and began to walk toward the front door of the shop. Just before they left, Estrella turned.

"Thank you, Mrs. MacGivor."

"And thank you, Estrella." She said the name loudly.

Except for the squeaking of the wheels and the sound of the horses' hooves, the trip to the glass house was utterly silent.

Estrella gasped as they turned into the long drive up to the glass house and she glimpsed the rose- and lavender-tinted gables. As more of the house became visible, it appeared like an enormous and rather gaudy chandelier. As they drew closer, it was as if a patchwork quilt of tinted light had been spread across the grassy meadow on which the house had been built.

"Splendid, is it not?" Lavinia's voice swelled with pride. "Four generations of Wickhams it's taken to build this house." She inhaled softly. "You might want to use these," she said, offering Estrella a set of dark spectacles.

"Why?" Estrella asked.

"The light can become awfully strong toward midday."

She took the spectacles but did not put them on. She wanted to see these colors with her naked eyes.

"The colors can glare quite fiercely in bright sunlight, or moonlight, for that matter."

I shall never put these on, Estrella thought.

The buggy stopped at the back door of the house, where what had once been a lovely garden was planted. Now, though, it looked as if it had suffered from neglect.

"That's the real garden over there." Lavinia pointed to

where a few hollyhocks and dahlias peeked over the top of a stone wall.

"The real garden?" Estrella was confused.

"Yes, it's glass. More than one hundred flowering plants, all hand-blown by us." She inhaled, and a blissful look crossed her face. "Exquisite!" she sighed.

Profane, Estrella thought. *Not natural*.

"Perfect," Lavinia murmured.

Depraved, Estrella concluded.

"Follow me," Lavinia Wickham said crisply. "I'll take you to your quarters."

Estrella looked toward the house, where her cousins Rose and Olivia leaned against a radiant glass shingle wall. With the black oval spectacles, they both appeared devoid of any resemblance to human girls. Their ages and their characters appeared blank, hollow. They were mere voids.

"This is Ella," their mother said as she led Estrella into the house.

"Most people just call me Estrella."

"We are calling you Ella," Lavinia replied sharply.

Of course. Why waste your breath on all those syllables? Estrella thought as they passed through the door. The two cousins followed.

They all walked into the house.

"No, not that way; upstairs is where your cousins sleep," Lavinia barked.

"Not simply cousins." Olivia scowled. "Third cousins."

"Forgive me, girls." Lavinia turned to Estrella. "We were very distant cousins with your grandfather and only through marriage, not really blood."

How reassuring, Estrella thought.

"You shall be sleeping in the cellar."

"It rhymes. Ella in the cellar." Rose giggled.

"But, oh, I nearly forgot." Lavinia raised a finger. "We have some settling to do. The household chores that I listed in my letter, you are to do every day—the cleaning and, most important, the maintenance of the garden. It is essential for attracting the small, lovely creatures Rose sketches for our glass figurines. You shall not be paid for those labors until you work off the debt you owe us."

"What debt?" Estrella asked.

"Your travel expenses, my dear. It was almost a four-hundred-mile journey, with so many stage stops and lodgings."

"Ten, in fact. But I thought my grandfather's solicitor had sent money to cover that."

"He had, but it was not nearly enough. You are here thanks to our generosity."

"But I don't understand—I still have almost a pound left."

"Well, hand it over, and I'll subtract that from what you owe us."

"Well, how much is that?"

"I don't know off the top of my head, but there were

other expenses in financing your trip here."

Estrella couldn't imagine what. She had bought the rubberized rain cloak but paid out of her own pocket for the sausage and cider, and her other meals.

"And what about my other chores? Am I to help you in the hot shop with the glassmaking?"

"Oh no! What would ever give you that idea?"

"Well, as you know, my grandfather was a lens grinder at the Royal Observatory. He made the lenses for the telescopes and repaired them as well."

"That is quite different from what we do here. Quite!"

"Yes, I would imagine so," she said softly.

18

THE SWAN AND
THE HEDGEHOG

That first night, after serving the family dinner and eating hers in the kitchen, she went to her cellar room. As soon as she got there, she unpacked her bag, and by some instinct she hid her two telescopes—the only things of real value she owned. One she put beneath her mattress in its case and the other into a cavity where she had discovered some loose bricks in the floor. She had moved her bed close to the single window well in the cellar. Then she propped open the rectangular window where, when darkness came, she would set up her telescope.

In half an hour, darkness had fallen. She took the refractor telescope from its hiding place. This scope had two lenses, one concave and one convex, to scoop up the light. Her grandfather had built it for her when she turned ten. She extended the scope to its full length, about two feet. She pointed it at the northeast corner of the sky. The lens toward the far end of the telescope scooped up the light, then bent it into parallel light rays, guiding it to the lens closest to her eye. "Ahh." She felt an incandescent light spreading within her as she saw the Cygnus, the swan constellation, rising and beginning its swim through the shoals of the Milky Way. She smiled as she recalled the myth of Zeus disguising himself as a swan to seek Leda, the wife of the Spartan king.

This was what Estrella loved about the stars. They held stories as well as codes, mathematical codes. The right ascension or angular distance to the east where Cygnus rose was 20.62. The declination measured north to south was 42.03. Love and passion, as well as numbers and distances—it was all there in the stars. She adjusted the focus, and the swan became sharper, but what about the space behind it? Tucked under the wing of the swan was a murky dark patch. Was this the nebula that her grandfather had suspected? He had glimpsed a bristle of stars buried near its edge. *Just like a hedgehog*, her grandfather had whispered. She had never seen him quite so excited. *Who knows what treasures it holds!* And by *treasures*, her grandfather did not mean stories or codes but universes, new universes. Now the bristles were becoming sharper. Could it be the hedgehog?

Two days later, Estrella stood in the garden with a cup of milk. "My! My!" she whispered in delight. The pumpkin she had planted appeared to have grown overnight and shined like a small moon in the garden. It had worked. One of the innkeepers she had met on her journey to the glass house told her that one needed to feed a pumpkin milk to make it grow. He had even shown her how to do it by cutting a small slit on the underside of a pumpkin vine and threading a wick through it to a cup of milk. As she was admiring the expanding contours of the pumpkin, she heard a soft chuffing sound nearby. She turned her head. A hedgehog stopped and looked directly at her.

"Oh my goodness! Hello there. You dropped down from the swan to say hello?" She extended her hand, palm up, to see if it would come. It did. The creature's bristles were relaxed and lay flat.

"Whatcha got there, Ella?" It was Olivia.

"A hedgehog."

"Well, put him in the cage for Rose to draw."

"Really?"

"What do you mean, really? Rose draws such creatures so Papa can make his glass animal collection. We're calling it the Wickham Glass Menagerie."

"But then what do you do with them?"

"We sell them," Olivia replied tersely.

"I mean the animals, not the figurines."

"We release them."

"Oh." Estrella paused. "I could help with that."

"No, you couldn't."

"Why not?"

"They . . . they . . . they get a bit confused. Rose is the one who knows just how to do it. Where to take them to make sure they can always find their way home . . ." She paused and looked straight into Estrella's eyes. "She has a way with animals."

It was a bald-faced lie, and Estrella knew it. But at the same time, there was a venomous glare in Olivia's pale gray eyes that said *Don't question me, you'll regret it!* Estrella gently picked up the small creature and put it in the cage. Olivia grasped the handle of the cage and stomped off toward the kitchen door.

That evening, when Estrella lifted the telescope to her eye, she looked for the swan again, and the nebula she thought she had seen tucked behind its wing. But she didn't see it, nor the next night. The time of the swan had passed, but Orion the warrior rose high in the night, flanked by other winter constellations.

Soon it would be the winter solstice, and the red planet, Mars, would begin to burn through the nights. Burn cold as the temperatures dropped. Tomorrow she would ask for another blanket and try to catch a mouse or squirrel for the cage. The Wickham menagerie was growing. The hedgehog had been a great success. They were planning a second edition. Every time Estrella caught an animal, Lavinia gave her a reward. An extra hunk of bread. A thicker pair of stockings. And maybe someday an extra blanket. Yes, a blanket! Would that be too much to ask for?

19

A SOB IN THE NIGHT

It had been late fall when Ulli had found the wanted sign. The owl had avoided telling Bess that he had flown over and found more wanted posters in other villages declaring Bess Wickham a witch. He would quickly tear them down. But now a bitter cold had settled upon the land. He was not worried for himself. Owls never get cold. Their thickly feathered bodies are well insulated. Yet he worried about Bess. But with her growing proficiency with the wand, she had practically made herself a new winter wardrobe. Nevertheless, one night it was so cold her teeth were chattering.

"I think you need to wand yourself up another layer of clothing and perhaps a blanket as well."

"Don't worry. I'm . . . I'm working on something." Ulli knew what this meant. He should be absolutely quiet. She was very still as she held the wand. There was a far-off look in her eyes and a tiny flicker, almost like a flame, at their very center. Before the owl realized what was happening, he felt the warmth, and then in the large hollow of the tree, where she had stacked some pinecones and dead leaves, there was a sudden kindling. Bess waved her wand once, then twice, and on the third time she blew softly and muttered some unintelligible words in a voice that Ulli had never heard. Small licks of flame suddenly appeared. Holding her wand high in the air, she exclaimed, "I did it! I did it indeed! I kindled the flame! I brought on fire!" She smiled at the wand and kissed its tip.

"What were those words you just spoke?" Ulli asked.

"I have no idea. They just came to me."

"Your voice was different."

"I know." Bess paused. "It wasn't mine."

"Well, whose was it?"

"I do believe it was Grannie's. Grannie's in the Summerlands."

"Summerlands? What is that?"

"I'm not sure, but she used to talk about the Summerlands sometimes. Never in front of my parents or sisters." She paused and scratched her head. I think it's something from long ago . . . in the time of the druids." Ulli suddenly seemed to grow very thin and quite tall. It was the owl's fear reaction, called *wilfing*. In a sense it was a camouflage strategy, which allowed him to blend in with a tree's trunk. It was as if the owl had erased himself and become part of the tree. The mention of druids always disturbed Ulli. There was talk that owls in the past had been druids—wingless mysterious creatures who seized human souls for their next life. Ulli stretched himself tall and zipped himself tighter into his own plumage.

Bess looked up at her old friend. "Don't worry, Ulli." She looked down at the wand and kissed it lightly. "Aren't we warm now? I'm getting better with the wand every day."

"That you are, my dear." But Ulli wondered about Bess's grannie. Had she been a druid?

The cold persisted for several days, and oftentimes, especially at night, the tree house became almost too warm for Ulli. So one evening the owl decided to fly over the glass house. It had been more than a year since Bess had left, and he was curious as to what her family was up to. His favorite perch for eavesdropping was by one of the chimneys for the hot shop, as voices rose on the waves of heat emitted from the furnaces.

On this night it was not voices he heard but a sobbing sound. He flew around the many gabled roofs and finally realized that the sobbing was emanating from the cellar. So Ulli settled on the ground, near the foundations, and began walking around the base of the house. There were many window wells. Ulli knew that these made sense, for the family must protect itself if a fire ever broke out. After all, heat rises, as do flames. The best way for a glassblower to escape if their house burst into flame was to crawl out through the basement—a window well sunk into the ground. But why would there be a person living down there now, in the coldest part of the house?

Ulli hopped into one of the wells. A guttering candle cast the shadow of a shivering girl hunched on a pile of rags.

Ulli scratched on the windowpane. The girl looked up. She was painfully thin and bedraggled. She came to the window and peered at Ulli. Could she speak? Ulli wondered. The only human Ulli could speak with was Bess. But maybe . . .

"Who are you?"

"Me?" The girl touched her chest lightly.

Ulli nodded.

"Ella—Ella in the cellar, they call me. But my real name is Estrella. My mamma named me for the stars."

"For the stars?" Ulli said. "How lovely."

They were conversing fluently. *How strange*, Ulli thought. Did the girl think this was odd?

"I can see the stars quite clearly on a night like this. And I brought my telescopes."

"Telescope? What's that?"

"An instrument, you know, for better seeing the stars."

She paused a moment. "Secretly, of course."

"Why secretly?"

"I feared they would take it from me if they knew." She paused. "They allow me few pleasures."

"And stars are your pleasure?"

"Oh, indeed." She tipped her head back and looked through the now-open window. She shivered but did not seem to mind the cold as she watched the silent march of the stars east to west across the blackness of the night. She began to whisper their names into the darkness. Vega, Deneb, Altair. They all shined resplendent like crystals in the air.

What a strange creature this girl was, Ulli thought. He was a creature of the night, with a lifetime of flying under these stars, yet he had never known their names.

Ulli flew off, but not before promising to return to visit the girl again. Estrella reached for her telescope and followed his flight until the owl disappeared into thick woods. She then tipped the scope toward the sky. Andromeda was rising. She spied the Chained Lady, one of her favorite constellations. Pressing against one side of the Chained Lady was her mother constellation, Cassiopeia, and to the other side, Pisces. Tears began to spill from Estrella's eyes. She remembered the story her grandfather had told her about the lovely Andromeda, who was captured and chained to a rock to be given as a sacrifice to a fiery sea monster. "Am

I to be that girl in chains? Will I be here forever and grow into the Chained Lady?" She slid her eyes up to the ceiling and thought of those monsters upstairs. What would they do with her?

Part Four

THE SILK

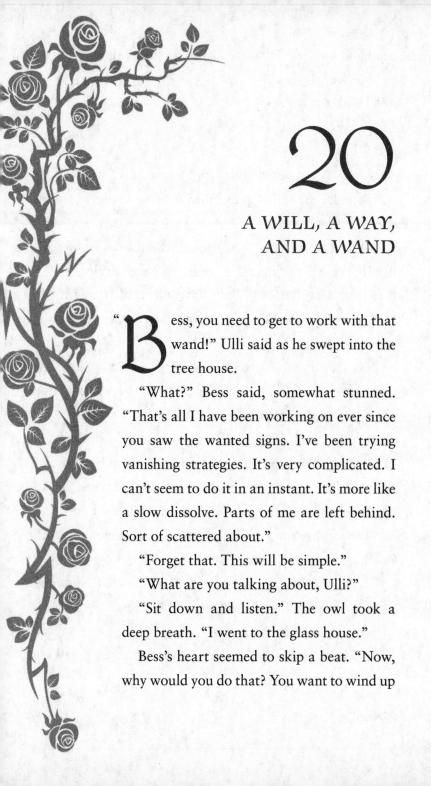

20

A WILL, A WAY,
AND A WAND

"Bess, you need to get to work with that wand!" Ulli said as he swept into the tree house.

"What?" Bess said, somewhat stunned. "That's all I have been working on ever since you saw the wanted signs. I've been trying vanishing strategies. It's very complicated. I can't seem to do it in an instant. It's more like a slow dissolve. Parts of me are left behind. Sort of scattered about."

"Forget that. This will be simple."

"What are you talking about, Ulli?"

"Sit down and listen." The owl took a deep breath. "I went to the glass house."

Bess's heart seemed to skip a beat. "Now, why would you do that? You want to wind up dead and soulless? How could you do such a thing?"

"No one saw me."

"That's not the point."

"But guess what? I saw someone."

"Who?"

"A girl. A girl about your age. Her name is Estrella."

"Estrella? I think I remember hearing about a distant cousin called Estrella."

"Yes, it means star. And she is not so distant now. She lives in the cellar of the glass house, and from the looks of it, they treat her miserably. Like a slave. Her clothes are threadbare. I don't think they give her much to eat. I can't imagine how she will survive this winter."

Bess stared at the lovely moss carpet she had made. The table now set with cups and saucers that she had conjured out of nothing with the wand.

"I . . . I could make some warm clothes, food, that sort of thing. And . . . and . . . you could carry it to her. But . . . but . . ." Bess's voice trembled. "It would be dangerous. If I could only master invisibility. That would be the best."

"The clothes must be invisible, too, or your family will become suspicious."

"True . . ." Bess's voice dwindled off. *Invisible clothing, now how could that be achieved?* "Nethers!" Bess whispered softly to herself.

"Nethers?" Ulli asked. "I have no idea what you're talking about."

"Nethers, underwear. Owls don't wear underwear. But humans do. It presses directly against their skin. It can't be seen because it is under all the outside clothes. I . . . I have a notion."

Ulli was excited. For whenever Bess said that word *notion*, it meant that she was focusing on the wand. She reached for the wand now. Rolled it between her palms and fixed her eyes on it. She seemed to peer into its very core. "Silk!" she exclaimed. "Spider silk! Of course." She looked up brightly at Ulli.

"Spider silk like the hummingbirds use in their nests?" the owl asked.

"Indeed!" Bess replied. Even before she had the wand, she had helped to weave spider silk into the hummingbirds' nests. Now she would make a whole suit of nethers for this poor girl, and a blanket as well. Spider silk was the best of all insulating materials. Every bit as good as wool. And who needed a spider when one had a wand?

Ulli watched quietly from a corner as Bess murmured a soft incantation. A large pile of silken thread soon emerged.

Bess now turned to Ulli. "Would you share a few of your plummels?" Plummels were the soft down fringe feathers of owls. They silenced an owl's flight and also had wonderful qualities of insulation. Perfect for nethers!

"Of course, dear. I'll be shedding them anyway in another month when spring comes." Ulli poked his beak into his primaries and a few plummels fell to the floor.

"That's enough," Bess said.

Another wave of the wand. Another distant look in Bess's green eyes, and soon there was a small mountain of downy feathers.

"Now what?" Ulli asked.

"I was afraid of this," Bess said despondently.

"Of what?"

"The wand never provides the whole solution."

"What do you mean?"

"I'm going to have to do the weaving, but I haven't a loom."

"So how . . . ?"

But Bess had already begun mumbling some incomprehensible words. And an odd contraption began to assemble itself.

"What's that?"

"A spinning wheel. I have to spin this silk and these plummels into threads. And then I can weave it. But I shall need a loom for that." She sighed.

But then, with a few more mumbled words, the loom appeared.

"My goodness," Ulli said, "that looks complicated."

"Not really. Grannie taught me how to spin." She reached down and took a clump of tangled spider silk. She rolled the wand over it. "See, now all the fibers are untangled. I'll be able to feed them into the spinning wheel to make the yarn."

Normally it would have taken longer, and she would have

needed carding paddles so all the fibers would be straight. But now there were no tangles, and she began feeding it onto the bobbin of the spinning wheel while she pressed her feet on the pedals at the base. Ulli watched as the wheel began to turn and the bobbin spun. What had been just a clump turned into thread. It did not take Bess long to spin the spider silk into neat balls of thread. It was almost as if her grannie were standing by her side with her hand on her shoulder, whispering a few words to her. *Hold it tighter and pedal faster, dear, makes the yarn feed into the wheel better . . . comes out smoother.*

"And now to work!" Bess announced. With a flick of the wand and a few muttered words, the warp of the loom was strung with crosswise strings of the silk thread. Then Ulli watched as Bess clasped a piece of wood and threaded some silk from the bobbin. The owl blinked as he saw Bess shooting the shuttle back and forth across the warp threads.

"Now, doesn't that look lovely. I'll have enough for a blanket and her underwear. As Grannie always said, 'Where there is a will, there's a way.'"

"A will and a way and a wand," Ulli said.

"Indeed!" Bess exclaimed.

It did not take long. The shuttle of the loom moved through the warp, and the silk moved like quicksilver.

"There!" Bess sighed when she had finished the blanket and the underclothes minutes later.

"Oh yes!" Ulli replied jubilantly. "I'll take it right to her."

"But you be careful. Remember, my father tried to kill you."

"Not something I'm likely to forget." Ulli sniffed.

He spread his wings and took off into the night with the blanket and the clothes.

Bess watched as Ulli dissolved into the night shadows. As she touched the wand to her lips, the wand became glass again. Would she be called a witch? Who decides who is a witch and who is not? Was her grandmother considered a witch? Yet her grandmother only did good things. Her grandmother gave to the poor, nursed the sick back to health. It was she who had taught Bess how to fix the broken wings of birds and feed orphan bunnies with a glass eyedropper. Was that kindly creature thought of as a witch?

Ulli perched on the edge of the window well into the cellar where Estrella slept. It was near dawn, and the candle in the room was just sputtering out. The fire in the grate was gone, with only ash left from the skimpy log they had allowed her. Ulli pecked on the window with his beak. It took the girl a minute to hear the sound. She looked at the owl at first with alarm but then with curiosity. Then she began to walk to the window. *How am I to explain this?* Ulli thought. As soon as the window was lifted, Ulli stuffed through the bundle.

"It's for you—take it. It will keep you warm." But the girl simply stared. Then Ulli extended his wing and brushed it softly against the girl's cheek. The girl's eyes closed as if she was feeling something absolutely marvelous. A hint of what was to come. The promised warmth. She took the bundle and unfurled it. First the quilt of spider silk, which she spread across her narrow bed, and then she unfolded the nethers. She slipped the leggings on. "Perfect fit," she murmured. Then she pulled on the top. "Aaaaah," she sighed. Ulli felt a twinge in his gizzard, where all owls feel their deepest emotions. A new sort of happiness flooded his being.

Estrella now came close to the window, looked deep into the black eyes of the barn owl, and whispered, "Thank you. Thank you from . . ." And she touched her heart and then touched Ulli's heart-shaped face. "From one heart to another." He plucked a small feather from his coverts, or tail feathers, and presented it to the girl. She tucked it behind her ear, and then something completely magical happened. The feather appeared to multiply into several others, and soon a cap of feathers fit snugly on her head. "I am warm!" she exclaimed. "Warm!"

Miles away, high in the oak tree, Bess peered into the dawn sky that was turning a rosy gold. Somehow, she knew. *We are warm now. All warm, be we bird or girl, beast or witch, we are warm.*

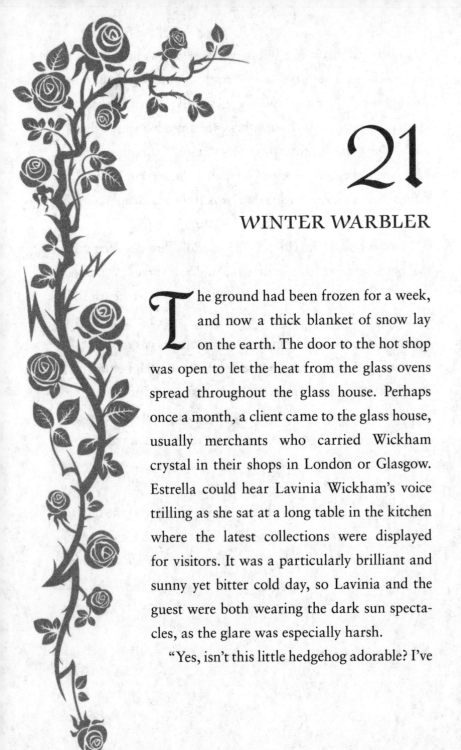

21

WINTER WARBLER

The ground had been frozen for a week, and now a thick blanket of snow lay on the earth. The door to the hot shop was open to let the heat from the glass ovens spread throughout the glass house. Perhaps once a month, a client came to the glass house, usually merchants who carried Wickham crystal in their shops in London or Glasgow. Estrella could hear Lavinia Wickham's voice trilling as she sat at a long table in the kitchen where the latest collections were displayed for visitors. It was a particularly brilliant and sunny yet bitter cold day, so Lavinia and the guest were both wearing the dark sun spectacles, as the glare was especially harsh.

"Yes, isn't this little hedgehog adorable? I've

nicknamed him Mr. Prickles. And let me show you something clever." From a deep pocket in her dress, she took out a quill.

"Is that a swan feather?" the visitor asked.

"Indeed, Mr. Lathem; a passing swan had a collision with a stagecoach a summer or so ago. He was beyond repair, but one of his feathers blew our way. And I whittled it into a pen. Now watch." She stuck the swan quill pen between the glass quills of the porcupine. "A perfect quill holder! Don't you think?"

"Absolutely!" the man exclaimed.

"Bet you could sell a lot of those."

"What happened to the rest of this poor swan?"

"Well, as I said. He was beyond repair. We brought the swan here. Laid him out on this very table. Even tried to give him a bit of spirits to revive the poor dear. But no, he was beyond hope."

"Beyond hope." The gentleman shook his head solemnly. "I am particularly fond of swans. Have you ever tried to cast a swan?"

"We find it easier to do smaller animals . . . easier to manage," she said softly.

Manage . . . manage how? Estrella thought. It was as if a dark shadow passed through her.

"But we are thinking of attempting to cast larger creatures. We have ordered a new, larger oven." She sighed contentedly and shut her eyes as if imagining this day.

"Well, if you're looking for small animals," the visitor offered, "I have heard that two new species of rabbits that were thought to be extinct are coming back."

"You don't say, Mr. Lathem? We have had great success with rabbits. What might these new species be?"

"The Angora rabbit from the time of Henry VIII, no less! The Angoras were not simply considered a lovely household pet but sought after for their marvelously soft fur. And the Dutch rabbit. Lovely mottled black-and-white fur. Said to love spinach. Plant yourself a spinach garden and of course some beets—they love beet roots—and you'll have Angora and Dutch rabbits hopping all over the place. Your daughter Rose will be sketching them all day long."

"Ella!" Lavinia Wickham called out.

"Yes, ma'am?"

"Where are you going?"

"Just to the garden to dig up some late parsnips and pota-toes."

"Might you also clear the front walk of snow? When cli-ents come, we don't want them to slip and fall."

"Oh, no problem," the gentleman said. He had gray, bushy sideburns and a thick but well-trimmed beard. "Now, is this your daughter who I once met?"

"Oh no, no . . . er . . . uh . . . Bess is off right now visiting an aunt in Burnham-by-the-Sea. This is Ella, our serving girl."

He stood up and came forward to shake her hand. "Hello, Ella, nice to meet you."

A look of alarm flashed through Lavinia's eyes.

"Nice to meet you, sir."

"And where are you from?"

"Greenwich."

"Ah, Greenwich. I used to go there often. There was another crystal shop there."

"Ah, Mr. Lathem!" Lavinia exclaimed. "I do believe I have another hedgehog in the back. I just recalled. They would make quite a pair, wouldn't they? Could be paperweights in addition to quill holders."

Mr. Lathem cleared his throat. "Ah yes, back to business. Indeed, the two would be nice, Mrs. Wickham." He now turned to Ella. "Nice to have met you, Ella." She was about to say, *My real name is Estrella*, but Lavinia Wickham gave her such a fierce look that she wrapped her shawl tighter and scurried out the kitchen door. The last words she heard were those of Mrs. Wickham. "A little slow in the head, if you know what I mean, so we can't have her working in the hot shop. Accidents happen, you know."

Just what kind of accidents happen? Estrella wondered.

Digging through the snow to find parsnips and potatoes was a cold job, as she couldn't wear her gloves to find them. She had to take several breaks to blow on her hands and warm them. Out of the corner of her eye she caught a glimpse of something bright red where the bean stakes still stood, the old stalks brown and winter burnt now. She walked over and crouched down. "A bird," she whispered. And not just any bird; a winter red-winged warbler! Was it dead? She scooped up the tiny body and blew her warm breath on it. Did she feel the dimmest quiver? Without a thought, she opened the bodice of her dress beneath her cloak and tucked the warbler against her chest.

This creature, she vowed silently, *is not going to be drawn by Rose.* She returned to the house and set the bag of parsnips and potatoes on the counter.

"And the walk, you cleared it completely?" Lavinia said.

"Yes, I need to change my stockings. They're wet."

"Well, after you change your stockings, I'd like you to walk to the far side of the glass garden. I have some ideas for staking out an area for a new vegetable garden. Say about twice as big as the one close to the house. There are some stakes stored by the cart in the barn."

Estrella now felt a distinct flutter of the warbler's wings against her chest. Once in her cellar room, she made a lovely little nest for the bird by unraveling some of the spider silk that Bess had used to make her underclothes and blanket. She then took some wood shavings from the tiny fireplace that she used to start her own fires. She packed them into a small bowl that could serve as a nest. She could feel the warbler beginning to stir a bit more as she shared the warmth of her own skin with the poor creature. There was just one thought that played through her head now. *Rose will not draw you . . . she will . . . not draw you ever!* The hedge-hog had disappeared forever, as had the butterflies and the hummingbirds last summer, and the kitten she found in the woodpile. There was something evil in this house. But this winter warbler would live to fly free again.

One afternoon, about a week after finding the warbler, Estrella came down to the cellar to put on a clean apron for serving dinner. She gasped with delight when she saw that the warbler was perched by the window. She had brought with her the small bits of food that she had been feeding the bird since she had found her—a handful of pine seeds and grain they had used to attract the birds to the garden, along with breadcrumbs, and any insect she could find in the house this time of year. Bugs seemed to be the warbler's favorite.

"My goodness!" she exclaimed in a whisper. "You want to fly, don't you? You have flown already in this dreary room." She looked to the corner where she had tucked the spider-silk nest. She went to the window and cranked it open. The warbler flew up onto her shoulder, then brushed her cheek with a red wing.

"You're saying goodbye, aren't you, dear?"

The warbler did not wait but beat its wings, and on a

light billow of wind floated out the window. Did she turn her head? Estrella couldn't tell because it had begun to snow heavily again, but she could see her bright red wings in the thickening flurries of snow.

"She is free! Would I ever dare leave? Would I dare to be free, too?" she whispered fiercely.

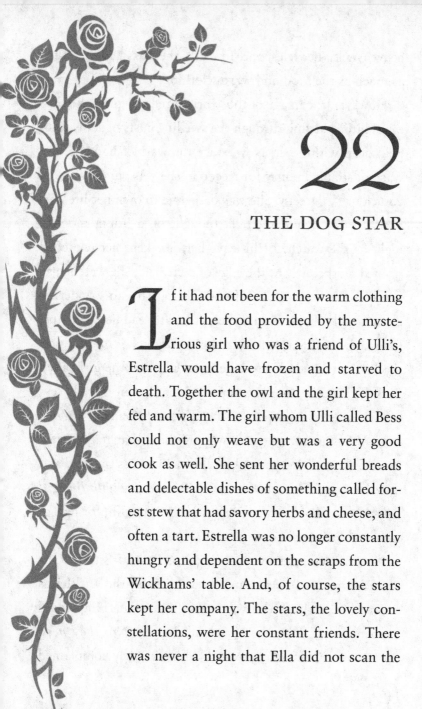

22

THE DOG STAR

I f it had not been for the warm clothing and the food provided by the mysterious girl who was a friend of Ulli's, Estrella would have frozen and starved to death. Together the owl and the girl kept her fed and warm. The girl whom Ulli called Bess could not only weave but was a very good cook as well. She sent her wonderful breads and delectable dishes of something called forest stew that had savory herbs and cheese, and often a tart. Estrella was no longer constantly hungry and dependent on the scraps from the Wickhams' table. And, of course, the stars kept her company. The stars, the lovely constellations, were her constant friends. There was never a night that Ella did not scan the heavens with her telescope. In truth, the stars kept her alive as much as the food and warm clothing.

However, the image of those bright red wings on the tiniest of birds battling through the swelling gusts of snow took hold deep within her. Now, since the warbler had left, she was not simply hungry for freedom, she was gluttonous . . . voracious . . . greedy. She was desperate to own her life.

Oh, to be a bird, Estrella thought on a bright moonlit night as she watched Ulli leave her. She kept her telescope trained on the owl. At the edge of a far field, she watched as Ulli dissolved into a thick forest. Estrella began wondering if she could follow. Should she ask Ulli to lead her? Perhaps, but maybe not. She sensed from the few bits of information she had managed to scrounge from Ulli that the girl called Bess did not like human company. It had taken Estrella several months to even pry her mysterious benefactor's name from Ulli. But tonight, she was thinking that maybe, just maybe, some night she might follow Ulli across the field and into the woods. *I could run away. I could live with this girl called Bess.* She dared not even suggest it to Ulli, for fear of what the owl would say.

Nevertheless, the owl was very protective of Estrella. She wasn't sure why. But Ulli knew how miserably the Wickhams treated her. Perhaps Ulli was fearful that something would happen to her. Was she herself in danger? *No, they need me too much*, Estrella reasoned. Although they complained constantly about how she could not tend the garden as well as "the previous girl." No, they never called her by name. Still, they needed Ella. She had brought them countless butterflies in the summer and even a wounded hummingbird one day. Rose would draw them, and after that Estrella never knew what happened to the creatures. She was only allowed in the hot shop to feed the fires and bellow the flames.

What had happened to those countless creatures she had brought for Rose's meticulous drawings? One day she asked to see those drawings and was told sharply that the sketches were always destroyed.

"Why?" Estrella asked.

"Someone might copy them. Our work is coveted; other glassmakers want to know our methods."

Nevertheless, the crystal hedgehog figurines began to haunt her, and those of the hummingbirds from summer, and a bright green frog she'd brought them, too. Where had they all gone once they were free? And what might happen to her if she simply ran away to that forest on the far edge of the field?

She began to think of running away constantly. It must be a moonless night, she decided. No chance of being followed. The days would be getting warmer. So possibly one night just after the last of the Worm Moon, that time of year when the earth begins to thaw, when life emerges and the ground can receive seeds. The moon is named for the worms that begin to emerge from the softening earth at that time. *Well, she thought to herself, this worm is coming out! This worm is escaping!*

The Worm Moon came and then began to wane, becoming thinner and thinner, and the ground softer and softer. Estrella's anticipation grew. The weeds in the garden were easier to pull, sprouts of radishes pushed their way up, and the worms seemed to push out of the ground as well. On the night of the last sliver of the Worm Moon, the constellation of the Dog Star rose, the brightest in the March sky. But it would not be fully visible until later in the evening.

Estrella had made her own star charts and timed the rising stars and constellations as carefully as possible. First, of course, was the Big Dipper; then she found Boötes in the Herdsman constellation. Finally, she saw Sirius, the Dog Star, the brightest, and its dim companion, a white dwarf star. As her grandfather had explained, *A white dwarf, Estrella, is a very dense star. It is composed of what we think of as very ancient matter. Large in mass but small in volume.* The memory of his musical voice filled her ears.

Estrella had a piece of paper that she scratched figures on, and with the small hourglass she had brought, she kept track of the Dog Star, Sirius. She knew precisely at what moment the brightest object in this March sky would slip away. And at that moment, she planned to open the well window in the cellar and slip out. She felt her heart beat rapidly as the sand drained. The top part of the hourglass was almost empty. She kept her eyes on it, but suddenly there was a strange green luminescence that streamed into the cellar. She looked up at the half-open well window. A savage face peered at her and growled. A wolf? The light in the creature's eyes blazed. The fangs glistened. Then a familiar voice.

"Come, come, Arwan. Don't wake the girl. Let her sleep. We have a lot of work for her tomorrow."

Estrella screamed. The dog slashed at the window with its paw. The window cracked. She would not think of escape again, not for a long, long time.

23

A LETTER TO GREENWICH

The nights flowed with stars, the shadowy clouds of unknown galaxies hung against the darkness like cobwebs in a boundless universe, daring Estrella's imagination.

Her dream of escaping did not die, despite the presence of the vicious dog, Arwan. But something else haunted her—it was the suspicion concerning the white dwarf star. She was obsessed with it. Had she seen what her grandfather thought he had spied just a year ago, three months before he died? She hesitated for several minutes but then picked up a pen and paper and began to write a letter.

❧

To the Keeper of the Lenses
The Royal Observatory
Greenwich, England

Dear Sir,

I had the extraordinary experience on March
22 of witnessing what I suspect to be a white
dwarf star, the possible companion star to the
Dog Star, Sirius. The right ascension or angular
distance to the east where it rose was 20.62. The
declination measured north to south was 42.03.
I observed this with a small telescope, the kind
made for home use, so I shall be the first to admit
that it can hardly compare to the Merz scope
at the Royal Observatory. But I observed the
white dwarf last year, with my late grandfather,
the previous lens keeper of the Merz telescope,
Barnaby Diggerton, and now this year I have
spotted it again on this very inferior telescope.
So that is why I am writing to you. I have been
hesitant to contact you because of my present
circumstances. I, of course, do not want to
distract you from your work, which is most likely
of much more vital importance.

I am sorry not to address you by your
Christian name, but I was never able to determine

who succeeded my grandfather as the keeper of
the lenses.

> *Most Sincerely,*
> *Estrella Diggerton*
> *Wickham's Fine Crystal*
> *Wee-on-the-Way, Crop Shire*

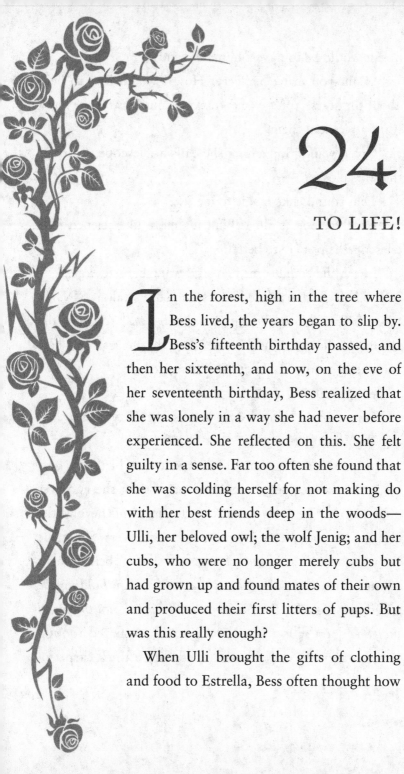

24

TO LIFE!

In the forest, high in the tree where Bess lived, the years began to slip by. Bess's fifteenth birthday passed, and then her sixteenth, and now, on the eve of her seventeenth birthday, Bess realized that she was lonely in a way she had never before experienced. She reflected on this. She felt guilty in a sense. Far too often she found that she was scolding herself for not making do with her best friends deep in the woods— Ulli, her beloved owl; the wolf Jenig; and her cubs, who were no longer merely cubs but had grown up and found mates of their own and produced their first litters of pups. But was this really enough?

When Ulli brought the gifts of clothing and food to Estrella, Bess often thought how nice it would be to have a human friend.

"Might you bring her here? How I would love to hear about the stars. You say she knows so much. And she has a wand to look at them."

"Not a wand. Something she calls a telescope. It brings the stars closer."

"That sounds like magic to me."

"No! No, not at all. I think it's more like science. The telescope helps her see better."

"I wish she could come here and bring her telescope."

But Ulli always refused and stomped his talons. "*Naich ti'han.*" This he translated to *Absolutely not.* "You want the family to follow her? And besides that, they have posted new wanted signs for you. So it's still dangerous."

Bess sighed. "What have I done now?"

"Oh, a barn burned over across the Way River, and they're blaming it on you."

And so, on the evening of her seventeenth birthday, Bess began to wander deeper into the wood than she had ever gone before. She soon came to a clearing, and beyond the clearing was a valley scattered with wildflowers. She made her way toward the birches. It was as if she was being drawn toward it mysteriously, almost magically. *I am holding the wand*, she thought. *But I command the wand, not the wand me!* She soon saw a small cottage with a curved rooftop beneath a grassy embankment, clad with a thick carpet of moss. The entry to the cottage was an arch made of birch limbs. The windows of the cottage were all round, as was the front door. On each side of the path to that front door, flowers spilled—toad lilies like small galaxies of stars, poppies, angel's tears, Queen Anne's lace.

Someone must be home, she thought as a twist of smoke rose from the chimney.

And at just that moment, she heard the creak of a door.

A tall young man stepped out. Hanging from his neck was an odd contraption. He raised it to his eyes and began to scan the horizon.

"By Jupiter, not a bird!" he exclaimed loudly, dropping the binoculars.

"Of course not!" Bess blurted out. "I'm . . . I'm a human. A human being." She had a brief and alarming thought. Had she mysteriously become an animal after living with them so long? No. She'd seen her reflection in a pond just the day before. She called up the pathway to the cottage, "I'm definitely a human being."

The young man was walking down the path. "A human being, a young lady." He thrust out his hand.

"Yes, I suppose so," she agreed softly.

She looked at the contraption hanging from a strap around his neck. "What is that?"

"Binoculars—somewhat newly invented. But perfect for people like myself."

"And what kind of person is that?"

"Ornithologist." Bess's face must have been sufficiently blank, because he quickly offered an explanation. "I am a scientist of birds."

"Oh," she replied softly, and remembered the other time she had heard that word. She was driving home from the village with her father, telling him about all the different kinds of hummingbirds. *Go on, girl*, her father had said. *You were rattling those names off like a veritable . . . what do they call it—ornithologist.*

"Well," said the young man. "It's simply that I love birds. I study them. Would you like some ginger mead?"

Bess hesitated. "Er . . . yes, I suppose so."

"My name is Will Darlington."

"Will," she repeated softly.

"And yours?"

It seemed as if her voice had become rusty after speaking only to animals for so long.

"Uh, just Bess."

"Just Bess! Lovely name." He flashed a smile. It took her a second or two to understand the joke.

"I . . . I . . . mean, just plain Bess." Then realized her mistake again. "Bess."

"This way, then, Bess." He gave a little bow and extended his arm toward the door.

The first thing she noticed was that all the windows were made of clear glass. There were no splashes of colored light on the floor. The light was clear as a mountain stream. The next thing that drew her attention was that every single wall was lined with books. She had never seen or imagined so many books in her life.

"Here, sit down. I'll make you a cup of ginger mead."

Actually, it had been so long since she had spoken to another human being that when the words first came out, she was not sure what language she was speaking. She stammered a bit.

"These . . . these . . . books, what's in them?"

"Well, mostly they're about birds. But I have a few volumes of poetry and history as well." He went to a nearby shelf and reached for one. "Here's one on African parrots."

"Africa! You've been to Africa." She caught her breath and looked at him. He had very black floppy hair that slashed across his forehead and kind brown eyes that sloped down a bit. His eyes almost seemed imploring to her, as if he were seeking her approval in some way.

"Yes, just once. Hope to go back to Africa sometime." He said this so casually, as if it was the most natural thing in the world. She could not help but wonder if anybody between Wee-on-the-Way and Glasgow had ever been to Africa.

In another minute he brought her a mug of ginger mead as she was paging through the book.

"Here you go," he said, setting down the mug.

"And what is this one?" Bess asked as she turned the page, pointing to a parrot with emerald-green feathers.

"Ah . . . a Cape parrot. Wonderful bird. The eyes are almost as green as yours." Bess felt herself blush. "So, Bess, where are you from?"

She was about to say Wee-on-the-Way, but then she recalled that Ulli had told her that there were new wanted posters up. What if Will had seen them and realized that he was serving ginger mead to a witch? "Oh, just around," she said vaguely. He did not press her. He seemed comfortable with her silences. She mostly talked to ask a question about the books she was looking at.

She had a second mug and then a third. Time seemed to melt away as she paged through his numerous books. The light coming through the clear panes shifted. She looked up suddenly. "Oh dear, I must be getting along."

"Wouldn't want to worry your family," Will said.

She looked up at him. "Of course not," she said softly. But she couldn't help wondering what he would say if he knew that her family consisted of a barn owl and several wolves. Then, to add to that, she lived not in a house or a snug cottage with hundreds and hundreds of books but rather in a great sprawling tree. For the first time in years, she felt rather freakish. Had she been away from the human world too long? But what choice did she have?

She got up to leave. In the doorway she turned to him. "Thank you, thank you so much for the ginger mead and for allowing me to look at your books."

"Please come back anytime." He paused. "Please do." He grasped her hand. *Hold my hand, hold it forever . . .* Bess thought, surprising herself. And she slowly pulled away, then turned and walked toward the valley below.

Will raised his binoculars and watched the slender figure until she reached the edge of the woods. He lowered his binoculars just as she turned to wave. "Take care," he whispered. "There are wolves in those woods."

And in that moment Bess seemed to sense what he was whispering. She felt tears spring to her eyes.

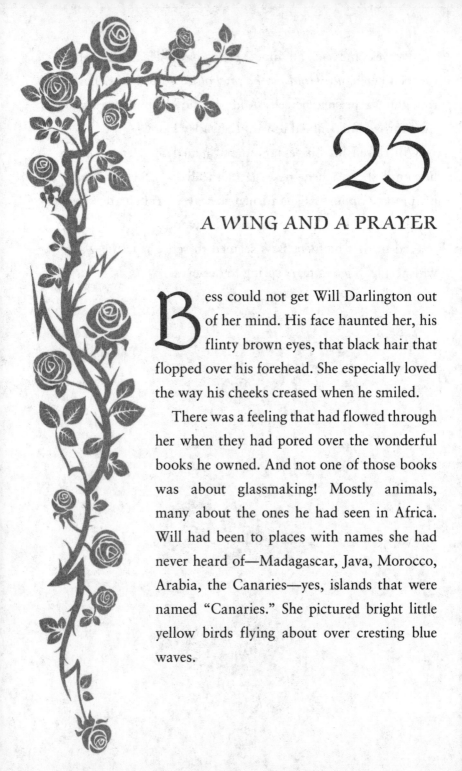

25

A WING AND A PRAYER

Bess could not get Will Darlington out of her mind. His face haunted her, his flinty brown eyes, that black hair that flopped over his forehead. She especially loved the way his cheeks creased when he smiled.

There was a feeling that had flowed through her when they had pored over the wonderful books he owned. And not one of those books was about glassmaking! Mostly animals, many about the ones he had seen in Africa. Will had been to places with names she had never heard of—Madagascar, Java, Morocco, Arabia, the Canaries—yes, islands that were named "Canaries." She pictured bright little yellow birds flying about over cresting blue waves.

His cottage was so cozy. Nothing like the vast and glaring glass house. He had spread a lovely cloth on the table, and even though the cups were chipped, she liked that. She had on occasion been to fancy houses of the people who bought Wickham glass, and their teacups were never chipped, and the tablecloths were embroidered with silver and gold thread. But Will Darlington's moss-covered cottage was entirely different. She wanted to see him again. Dare she go uninvited? And then if she did go, he might expect her to invite him back to her house. But wouldn't he think the fact that she lived in a tree very peculiar? Especially with an owl and a family of wolves as her only nearby companions. Would it lead him to ask too many questions? Once again, the dreadful thought came into her mind. It was as if a storm cloud passed over her, eclipsing all the good she had just felt. What if he had seen the witch posters? Ulli said he had torn down as many as possible, but there was still a chance that Will had seen them. And if he had, what would he say? *You remind me of someone.* And then what would she answer, ever so casually? *Ah yes, I'm the witch of Crop Shire . . .*

She rested her chin in the palm of her hand and tried to conjure up his face again. The tousled hair, the lovely creases that framed his smile, his voice. His voice was the most elusive feature of all. She who could remember every call of every bird could not quite recall his voice. Was it soft? Not exactly. Leathery? A bit, perhaps.

For two days, Will was all she thought about. Finally, on the third day, Ulli, who had been watching her carefully, came to a conclusion. Bess had fallen in love. He stepped up to the small table in the hollow where Bess was once again daydreaming and spoke.

"Write him!"

"Write who?"

"Don't play dumb with me. Write the lad." And with that, he plucked a feather from his own body.

"What lad?"

"I might not be human, but I'm wise. Isn't that what they always say? Wise old owl. And now I have been hopeful enough and silly enough to pluck one of my own primaries for you to write with."

"Oh dear!"

"No *oh dear*s, just write to him. And I'll take it."

"But you don't know where he lives."

"You can tell me. Now WRITE."

It would take her three days to write the letter.

At dawn, Will Darlington stepped out of the moss-covered cottage with his binoculars and scanned the eastern horizon as the sun rose, turning the first shades of lavender to pink. Then against the pink was the wingspan of what he was certain was a barn owl, for they were pale, almost white, and tipped in darker tones. "Why now?" he whispered to himself. For it was an odd time, daybreak, for an owl to fly.

The owl came closer and then, angling its wings, began to bank steeply. He now noticed that the bird had something clapped in its beak. Soundless, it glided in and set down on a rock nearby. Then, stepping off the rock, it began to walk toward Will. In all his life, Will had never had an animal from the wild directly approach him. But this creature did. It tipped its head down and dropped a rolled piece of paper at Will's feet. He bent down and picked it up. Unrolling it, Will began to read. Dare he even hope that it could be from the girl who had found her way to this house? Who had pored over his books and asked not simply good questions, but often profound ones?

> *Dear Will,*
>
> *My afternoon with you was so much more than just an afternoon. I felt as if I had broken through into an entirely new world. I can recall every book, every page of every book that I looked at with you. And now I have a question. Do you recall your book* Wading Birds of the Southern Hemisphere? *Birds like the beautiful roseate spoonbills of southern climes. Why is that bird's beak indeed shaped like a spoon?*
>
> *I have a few more questions as well.*

She then listed twenty-three questions concerning at least eighteen different species of wildlife.

And closed the letter:

> *Yours respectfully,*
> Bess

Will Darlington sat down at his desk, pulled out a sheet of very coarse paper, and wrote back.

> *Dear Bess,*
> *The roseate spoonbill's beak was designed by the good Lord so that it could scoop up the delectable delights of the shallows without ever having to dip its head under the water—sand crabs, minnows, shrimp, aquatic insects, etc. But to answer all your questions about the eighteen other species of animals you have inquired about, I think you need to come again to my cottage for some ginger mead—soon!*
> *Yours,*
> Will

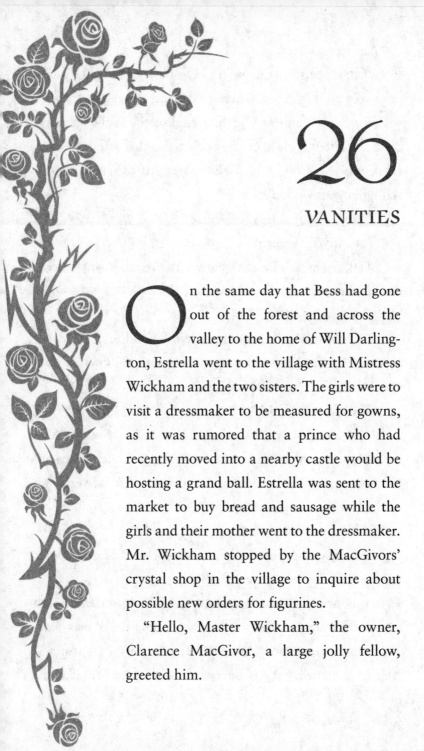

26

VANITIES

On the same day that Bess had gone out of the forest and across the valley to the home of Will Darlington, Estrella went to the village with Mistress Wickham and the two sisters. The girls were to visit a dressmaker to be measured for gowns, as it was rumored that a prince who had recently moved into a nearby castle would be hosting a grand ball. Estrella was sent to the market to buy bread and sausage while the girls and their mother went to the dressmaker. Mr. Wickham stopped by the MacGivors' crystal shop in the village to inquire about possible new orders for figurines.

"Hello, Master Wickham," the owner, Clarence MacGivor, a large jolly fellow, greeted him.

"Any new orders, sir?"

"Well, it's too bad that wolf's head blew up on you. Could have sold a lot of those. What was it, three years ago now?"

"Erm, yes," Charles Wickham said softly, as the memory of the shattering glass head ricocheted in his mind. "A difficult process. You know." He cleared his throat. "What's selling now, my good man?"

"Your hummingbirds, of course."

"Yes. Anything else?"

"Well, there's a new glassblower in Glasgow who's been doing what are called vanities."

"Vanities?"

"Yes, especially crafted for ladies' boudoirs. Delicate, feminine figures from grand duchesses to milkmaids and shepherdesses. Quite the fashion."

"How does he do it?"

"A she, sir. A woman. It's done by mold blowing. She fashions them in clay casts, a two-part mold, then blows in the hot glass. Similar to what you do for your flowers and birds. Her detailing is exquisite."

"Might I see one?"

"Certainly." He reached into a cupboard and brought one out. "I like this one especially."

It was of a shepherdess standing with her staff in hand and a charming bonnet on her head. The dress was pale blue with a white apron, and her feet were bare. "Charming, isn't it? I like that she is barefoot, as you can see. It adds something to it, I think. Although I don't know why a shepherdess would be barefoot. But very fetching."

"Yes, very," Charles said. "Quite lovely."

Mrs. MacGivor now came from the back office. "Ah, Mr. Wickham, how are you on this beautiful day?"

"Grand, Mrs. MacGivor. Just grand." He could barely take his eyes from the lovely shepherdess.

"And how is that nice girl who's helping you and the missus out?"

"Oh, good enough, I s'pose."

"Just 'good enough'?"

"A little slow in the head and ornery on occasion."

"I'd never believe it!"

"Oh, you better believe it!"

Mrs. MacGivor gave him a narrow look. He did not seem to notice, as his eyes were still fixed on the figurine of the shepherdess. "Slow in the head?"

"Yes. I hope she makes it back to the cart. But Mrs. Wickham is keeping an eye on her."

At this very same moment, Estrella was delighting in being able to come to town with them and scanning the route for any possible escape. As she rounded the corner, she came upon a streetlamp with a wanted sign. She stopped to read it. Opening her eyes wide, she gasped. *Bess Wickham!* The sister they never talked about—Bess! Ulli's Bess? A witch! She knew that Wee-on-the-Way was not like Greenwich, a sophisticated center of learning and science. But did the people actually believe in witches? Witches were a thing of the past, a hundred years or more ago. The drawing of the girl did bear a resemblance to her sisters, except this girl had a kindness in her eyes. More likely that Rose and Olivia were witches than this girl.

Preoccupied with her thoughts, she continued on and was so distracted that, before she knew it, she found herself at the cart with the family. The girls were chatting furiously about the gowns they had ordered. "Pink silk!" Rose sighed. "Pink goes with my complexion, and my name, of course."

Lavinia tipped her head. "Yes, I suppose so." But she really wasn't looking at her daughter but at Ella. Ella in the last few months had indeed grown quite pretty. Plumper, and in fact rosier. She glanced at her own daughters. They seemed thin and rather sallow in comparison. Had Charles noticed?

Later that evening, as they prepared for bed, Lavinia turned to her husband. "Charles, have you noticed that Ella has become plumper and more rosy-cheeked?"

"Has she?"

"Indeed. I try not to indulge her too much. When one begins to indulge servants, it never works. They get too sure of themselves, even haughty."

"Do you think she's stealing from the larder?" her husband asked.

"I don't know," Lavinia said slowly. "I don't understand it. I keep her mostly on gruel and the scraps from our own dinner plates."

"We have to save every penny, as our sales are down. Ella's gardening does not attract the creatures that Bess's did," her husband replied.

"Well, Bess was a witch. So what do you want? A witch or a full-cheeked, rosy girl?"

"Don't be ridiculous, Lavinia. One witch in this family was enough." Charles shut his eyes tight. He was still haunted by the luminous green eyes of that wolf. So like his daughter's.

"Lavinia, remind me, did your mamma, Grannie, have green eyes?"

"Yes, she did. I think it has been said that green eyes skip a generation. None of the other girls have them."

"Only Bess," Charles replied ominously.

It was just a few days later that Charles came from the hot shop and as he passed the counter where new pieces were set, he glanced out the window. Framed in that blue-tinted window was Ella in the garden with her rake. The picture she made was arresting. The sun was high in the sky, and she was warm. She had stopped and leaned on the hoe and tipped her bonneted head up. Charles inhaled sharply. It was as if that figurine he'd seen in the crystal shop in

Wee-on-the-Way had come to life. "Exactly," he murmured as he glimpsed Ella's bare feet.

For the next several days, Estrella felt as though she was being watched constantly by Charles Wickham, which left her feeling unsettled.

And indeed, there were so many instances over the days that followed when Charles would glimpse her and think, *Perfect!* Once she was down by the pond, having gone for a swim, and was resting on the banks. She could have been a mermaid on the beach, Charles Wickham thought. Her hair was in long, amber-colored tangles. Her legs, now crossed at the ankles, could have melted into a mermaid's tail with glittering iridescent scales. Another time he caught sight of her coming through the field with a lamb in her arms.

He came out from behind a tree as he spied her, and she gave a start.

"Whatcha got there, girl?"

"Uh, Farmer Buckham's lamb got out of the lambing pen somehow. I'm just taking it back."

Charles Wickham was silent for almost a full minute, just staring at her. The lamb began to wiggle.

"I better be on my way," she said, "or he'll escape again."

"Yes, yes. Of course."

She continued walking. But she could feel his eyes on her back.

Charles Wickham turned and headed back to his house, deep in thought.

"Lavinia!" he cried out as he came through the door. "Lavinia!"

"Just in the back room, Charles."

He entered the room and looked at the recent work, all of it remarkable—bunnies, fox kits, a few hummingbirds.

"Lovely, aren't they?" Lavinia said.

"Yes, yes, my dear, but we have expanded the editions and they can no longer be considered limited. We used to get twenty-five pounds for a figurine, and now we get barely three. Our profit margins have gone down considerably. Less money for more work. Barely covers the cost of stoking the ovens."

Lavinia sighed. She knew her husband was right. "We need something new, I suppose."

"Exactly. Grab your hat, my dear. We have to go to town."

"Where are we going?"

"MacGivors'."

"But we don't have an order from them. Haven't in months."

"I want to show you something. Be quick now. Get your bonnet or you'll be red as a beet. The sun is fierce today."

"Come in, come in," a voice cried out as the bell rang, announcing the Wickhams' arrival at the shop of MacGivor & Sons fine crystal and glassware.

"Ah, the estimable Charles Wickham and the lady

Wickham. What can I do for you today?" Clarence Mac-Givor greeted them.

"Mr. MacGivor, would you do me the good favor of showing my wife those exquisite glass figurines—the vanities, as you call them?"

"Ah, the vanities, of course. The edition has already sold out of the shepherdess and the duchess. But I keep one of each for display purposes. The windows change tomorrow, and as soon as I put them in, you'll bet the next edition will sell out as well. Let me fetch a couple."

As Mr. MacGivor disappeared into a back room, Charles turned to his wife. "Lavinia, wait until you see this!"

MacGivor was back within two minutes. Carefully he unwrapped the figurines.

"And here is your shepherdess." He set the figure on the countertop. Lavinia gasped. "And now for your dairymaid, with a bucket of fresh milk."

She leaned down and examined the two figures closely. "Look! Look at that. Oh, those bare feet are the perfect touch. And the way she is holding the staff. And the milkmaid, too. Yes, yes. Simply exquisite."

"They are the latest rage, Mrs. Wickham. It seems like the gentry have a penchant to see their servants immortalized. Enough of these Napoleonic generals and king's grenadiers or birds and bees. The delights are closer to home—in their own backyards, so to speak."

Wickham regarded his wife closely. She was clearly impressed. But did she know what he was imagining? He would have to tread carefully.

They left the shop and walked silently to where they had parked the buggy, instead of the cart. The Epson buggy only held two people and had fine leather seats. It was the appropriate vehicle for an outing of some import. And this was such an outing. Charles Wickham was nervous. He was not sure how to open this conversation. His eyes narrowed as he slid his gaze toward his wife.

"Well"—he exhaled a breath—"what do you think?"

"I think we should go to Mrs. Himmleworth's and buy a new bonnet for Ella and a new blue servant's dress and an apron."

"Oh, my dear! Praise be! This is our future."

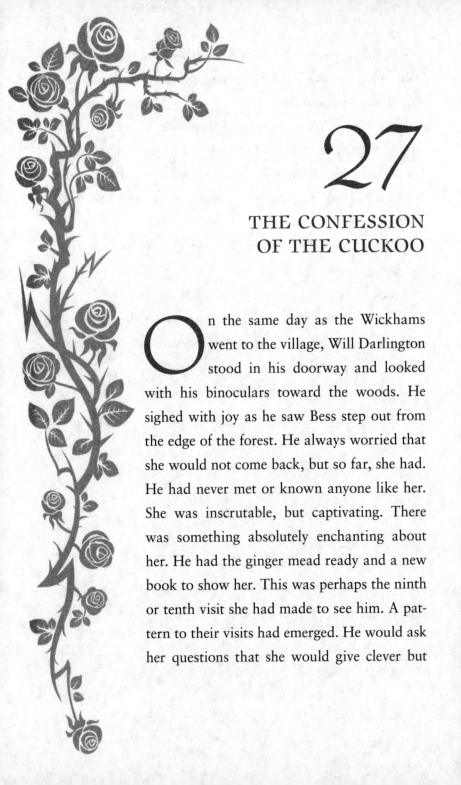

27

THE CONFESSION
OF THE CUCKOO

On the same day as the Wickhams went to the village, Will Darlington stood in his doorway and looked with his binoculars toward the woods. He sighed with joy as he saw Bess step out from the edge of the forest. He always worried that she would not come back, but so far, she had. He had never met or known anyone like her. She was inscrutable, but captivating. There was something absolutely enchanting about her. He had the ginger mead ready and a new book to show her. This was perhaps the ninth or tenth visit she had made to see him. A pattern to their visits had emerged. He would ask her questions that she would give clever but elusive answers to, and she would ask him questions that he would give amusing and direct answers to. Although there were some answers he gave that perhaps were not so direct.

"Where were you born, Will?"

"In my mother's bed on the Isle of Skye. And you, Bess?"

Her eyes would twinkle.

"Well, Will, actually I wasn't born. I was hatched, so to speak."

"So to speak?" His eyes crinkled.

"Yes, do you know about the cuckoo bird?"

"You mean the *Cuculus canorus*," he replied, giving the scientific species name.

"Is that Latin for cuckoo bird?"

"Yes."

"Indeed, I am learning a lot of Latin these days." She smiled and took a deep breath. "Well, you know how the cuckoo lays its eggs in another bird's nest?"

"Yes, I know about that. The eggs are larger than the host bird's own eggs but very similar in coloration."

"So it is with me."

A shadow of concern swept across Will's eyes. "What do you mean?"

"I was put in the wrong nest." She paused and then grinned.

"What the devil are you talking about?"

"Just what I said. I was put in the wrong nest, so I left."

"B-b-b-but . . . but when? When you were a baby?"

"No, not that young. I really can't remember now. Maybe three years ago."

"But where did you go?"

"To friends. They take good care of me." She added, "And I of them." Then she turned toward the bookshelves. "Do you have any books on cuckoo birds?"

"Most likely. But I've been rearranging things. I'll make us a cup of tea, and if you go into my study and look on that first shelf, I think to your right there are at least a half dozen."

A half-dozen books on cuckoo birds! Bess thought to herself. *Imagine that!* This was an absolute treasure house, and Will was the best treasure in it. She paused a second as she walked into the study and thought how lucky she was to know this charming person, a good person! She felt a bit of a flutter every time they were together.

Meanwhile, Estrella walked into the cellar of the glass house and saw that a brand-new bonnet and work smock with a crisp white apron had been laid out for her. Her own clothes were in shreds except for the warm spider-silk underclothes that Ulli had brought for her. Her room, in fact the entire glass house, seemed extremely warm, much warmer than usual. It certainly wasn't hot outside. She wasn't sure what accounted for it.

"It seems unusually warm in here," Estrella said later that day. Olivia and Rose exchanged glances. Rose suddenly smiled brightly—too brightly. Their teeth gleamed; their eyes glittered with a voracious glow.

"Oh, don't you look nice in that new dress!" Rose exclaimed.

"Pretty enough for a picture!" Lavinia exclaimed. They were all smiling too much.

"Rose should sketch you."

"NO!" Estrella exclaimed.

"Why ever not?" Olivia asked.

"I just don't want to. That's all."

"We could pose together in the swing."

"I'm not an animal," Estrella said firmly.

"Nor am I," Olivia replied.

No more was said for several days, but she did notice Rose staring at her quite frequently, and once she saw a silverpoint pencil fall from a deep pocket in Rose's dress. She felt as if she was being stalked. Not only that, but Arwan, the dog that had barked furiously at her the night she had planned to escape, seemed to follow her everywhere now.

She was never permitted into the studios where the ovens were. Most of her information came from dinner table conversation that she picked up when she was serving the family. But it was quite technical. There had been quite a bit lately about the new, larger oven that they had ordered and was expected any day now.

"For the gathering oven, I would recommend a mixture of pine and oak," Charles Wickham said. "Makes for a good, even temperature for larger objects. We'll need at least twelve pounds of blue cristallos." He glanced at Estrella's dress as she took a platter back to the kitchen. "And that takes at least six days to come up to temperature. The reheating chamber ovens do not require as much time as the annealing fires to reach proper temperatures."

Then another evening as Estrella cleaned up in the kitchen, she heard the Wickhams discussing more business. "Charles, I've been struggling with this order from Amsterdam, and I'm confounded. The pound to guilder rates have changed again. I can't figure it out."

"Ask Ella. She did the conversion on the last exchange with Amsterdam."

"Ella!" Lavinia called out.

Within scant minutes, Estrella had figured out the exchange rate and the cost for shipping the package to Amsterdam. Lavinia didn't thank her but just nodded rather grimly and said, "You have a way with numbers." Then added softly, "An unnatural way."

Estrella looked at her, unsure what she meant. "I was taught by my grandfather."

"He taught you, did he?" Then, barely pausing, "What else did he teach you?"

"I . . . I . . ." she stammered. "I don't know what you mean."

But Lavinia had already turned her back and walked out of the room.

Part Five

THE MAKING
OF A WITCH

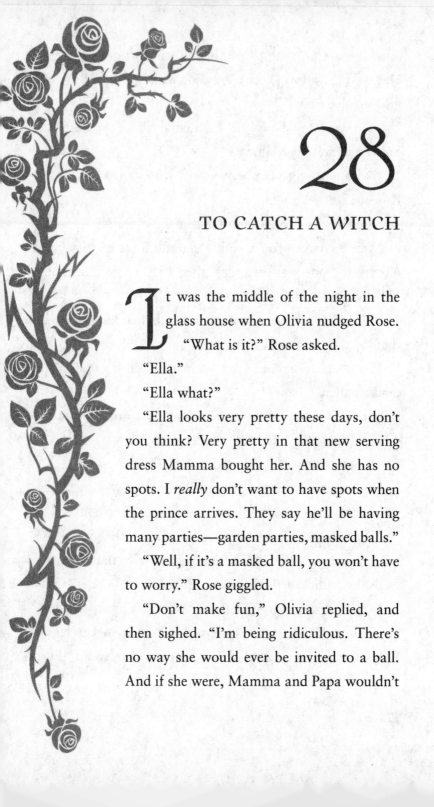

28

TO CATCH A WITCH

It was the middle of the night in the glass house when Olivia nudged Rose. "What is it?" Rose asked.

"Ella."

"Ella what?"

"Ella looks very pretty these days, don't you think? Very pretty in that new serving dress Mamma bought her. And she has no spots. I *really* don't want to have spots when the prince arrives. They say he'll be having many parties—garden parties, masked balls."

"Well, if it's a masked ball, you won't have to worry." Rose giggled.

"Don't make fun," Olivia replied, and then sighed. "I'm being ridiculous. There's no way she would ever be invited to a ball. And if she were, Mamma and Papa wouldn't allow her to go." She paused. "And what would she wear? Her serving uniform with a dazzling white apron?" Both the girls giggled now.

"Did you see how she calculated those figures, the exchange rate, for Mamma?"

"Does a young man want a girl who can do figures?" Rose asked.

"Probably not. It's unnatural, as Mamma said."

"Yes, I suppose you're right. Unnatural for a girl who is our age to know figures and mathematics. I mean, Mamma only knows because Papa taught her."

"Well, Ella said her grandfather taught her. He worked at the Royal Observatory, Papa said."

"But that's just about stars. Stars have nothing to do with mathematics."

"Yes, I doubt that stargazing does have anything to do with mathematics. Not real mathematics."

"What exactly are real mathematics?" Rose asked.

"I'm not sure, but the other day I saw her writing something down in a little book that she keeps in her pocket."

"Does she always keep it in her pocket?" Rose asked.

"I think so," Olivia said. "And what about that milk she feeds the pumpkin? Is that not strange?"

"The dark arts, I think," Rose replied in a husky whisper.

Olivia rolled over and propped her head in her hand. "Maybe she keeps other things in her cellar room? Ever think of that, Rose?"

"Maybe . . ." Rose replied slowly, and slid her eyes toward her sister Olivia. "We could find out, you know."

"I bet we could!"

Ever since Mr. Lathem had mentioned the return of the Dutch and the Angora rabbits to vegetable gardens, Mrs. Wickham had been determined to build a new garden—the spinach garden, they called it. It was not easy work, and Charles Wickham had joined Estrella to help her dig out the ground that was to be the site of the new garden.

They were both hot. He had taken off his work jacket to hang it on the fence. He rested one arm on a fence post and looked at Ella, who had flung back her bonnet so that her hair that had come free of its braids was blowing in the wind. What a sight she made—*A vanity like no other!* he thought.

But for now, they must get the garden ready to plant. *The rabbits will come*, he thought. The fires that had been snuffed because business had been so slow would gain strength again, and amazing new editions would be cast.

Estrella turned suddenly and faced him. It was as if she had felt his eyes drilling into her back. From her own eyes there was an accusatory blaze of light. "Why do you stare at me so?" she said in a low, dangerous voice. He muttered something that was inaudible and went back to work with his hoe.

೧

It was at least two hours later when she returned to her cellar room. As soon as she opened the door and stepped in, she knew that something was different. Someone had been in her room. She could feel it. She had so few possessions: a few books, an hourglass, just enough clothes to hang on a single hook. But something was different. Her two telescopes! Her heart leaped as she thought of the two scopes hidden away. She ran to the foundation wall, where she dislodged the brick that hid one scope. The Janssen scope was still there. She swiveled around and looked at her bed. The bedcover was slightly disturbed. Her heart began to thump wildly in her chest. Ripping the cover off, she stared down at the pile of shattered glass—the glass lenses of the telescope had been smashed to bits. The metal parts, no longer intact, lay like severed limbs of a once-beautiful whole.

She heard something behind her. Turning around, she saw the smirking faces of Olivia and Rose.

"Witchery!" Olivia hissed.

"Positively hek-ish!" Rose added.

"Why? Why?" Estrella raged at them. "What do you want from me?"

"It's quite simple." A thin-lipped smile crawled across Rose's face.

"What?"

"You see, Ella, today a courtier from the prince's palace is to come with invitations to a ball. You need to be out of sight for the rest of the day. We thought a little project might help occupy you."

"Such as fixing your witch's tool." Rose sniggered.

The two sisters turned and left the cellar.

Estrella was aghast. She crumpled to the floor, sobbing.

29

A SOUL FREED,
ANOTHER TRAPPED

In a distant valley far from the glass house, Bess was relishing the charming house of Will Darlington. But then she began to tremble. "Stellina!" Bess gasped as she looked at the crystal figurine of the hummingbird. "Evil man!" she screeched as Will ran into the study. He could not believe his eyes. Bess—his lovely Bess—had been transformed into a raging creature.

"What? What in heaven's name?"

"Don't you dare take another step."

"What happened?"

"This happened." She withdrew the wand from the fold of a hidden pocket in her dress and pointed it at the glass figurine of the hummingbird. "Her name is Stellina."

Bess wasn't sure how it came to her, but she began whispering some words—charm words that she had never used before—and suddenly there was the sound of shattering glass. And then it was as if a living rainbow had swirled up into the air. The radiant wings of Stellina shimmered, and the ruby-throated hummingbird flew out the open window. Bess was stunned and felt a weariness wash over her. Her heart was thunderous in her chest. Something odd was happening to her. She looked at her hand that held the wand, but it was as if she were looking through air. She felt a tingling as she glanced at her feet, which felt like they were on the ground but weren't. *What is happening to me?* she wondered. *I am melting away. The invisibility spell is working!* she thought as she watched her other hand dissolve into thin air. There was a strong gust of wind, and Bess vanished entirely right before Will Darlington's eyes.

In the cellar, Estrella's pillow was soaked in tears. She wished that Ulli were here. The owl had truly become her closest friend. Her only friend. Ulli still told her stories about the mysterious girl, Bess, who lived in a tree in a distant forest and spoke the language of many creatures.

"Why can't she come here and visit me?" she had asked Ulli dozens of times. But Ulli was always evasive.

Now, as Estrella sat resting her chin on the windowsill, she spied something in the sky. She squinted and began to make out a familiar form.

"Ulli!" she whispered. Had she wished the owl here in some desperate way?

Ulli in the meantime had dipped low as he caught sight of three men on horseback in the royal livery of the prince's colors. *Ah, the ball,* Ulli thought. And a perfect time to visit Estrella, as the Wickhams would be keeping her out of sight. It was odd, Ulli reflected, how the daughters had grown uglier and yet Estrella more beautiful. A sudden ruffle of fear stiffened his primary feathers.

Ulli began to carve a steep turn. As he took off toward the glass house, he could see Estrella looking up through the cracked cellar window. He settled on the edge of the window well.

"Hello, Estrella. I came to check on you." The owl held up one talon in the air. "Wait, let me guess. The prince's messengers have come to deliver an invitation to a ball, and your masters want you out of sight."

"Yes, so they told me," Estrella replied. Ulli cocked his head. He could see that Estrella had been crying.

"All right, dear, now tell me what happened."

Another torrent of tears burst from Estrella's eyes.

"What could possibly be so terrible?"

The story of the broken telescope tumbled out in broken pieces as jagged as the smashed lenses of the scope.

"How could they?" Ulli gaped at the fragments. "Have you told their parents?"

"No. The Wickhams wouldn't care. They are as heartless

as their daughters."

"They could mend the lenses for you. They're glass-makers."

"They wouldn't ever."

"But I see they've started the glassmaking fires again," Ulli said. "Business must be improving."

"I guess," Estrella said, whimpering. "But they're worried, as the fires are slow getting up to temperature. I feel I have shoveled enough coal and chopped enough wood for an entire village. That's the only thing I am permitted to do in the hot shop: feed the fires in the ovens. They have a new oven that is quite large and will take forever to get hot enough."

"Hot enough for what?"

"I don't know—a large animal. Or perhaps a small elephant." She laughed.

Ulli did not laugh. He felt a deep twitch in his gizzard. A terrible thought streaked through Ulli's mind. He had never divulged the dreadful maze of mirrors that the Wickhams used for extracting animals' souls.

Estrella sighed. "Just look at me from tending those ovens." She twirled around. "My work smock is stained with smudges from the ashes." She rustled the skirts. Cinders sprinkled out from the hem. "Not quite fit for a prince. But I do have a brand-new dress for serving. She nodded to the blue frock and white apron and bonnet hanging from a hook.

Estrella gasped as she saw Ulli stretch taller and within seconds become very thin.

"What's wrong with you?"

Ulli blinked. How did one explain wilfing, the fear reaction of owls? He recalled his nighttime visit to the village and seeing the vanity figurines in the window of the Mac-Givors' fine crystal shop. There had been a fetching figurine of a shepherdess in a blue frock with a white apron and bonnet, just like the one hanging on the hook in Estrella's room. A terrible image began to form in Ulli's mind. The owl flew off urgently, without an excuse for his sudden departure.

30

A CALL TO ACTION

U lli flew into the tree house. Bess was still asleep. Ever since she had returned from the far valley where she visited the moss house, Bess had been in a state. She would explain nothing but simply crawled into her bed and pulled up the covers. Ulli heard her weeping at night, sometimes pounding her pillow and muttering, "How could he? Monster . . . beast." It didn't take Ulli long to guess what had happened.

"All right, quite enough!" Ulli hooted and tore the blanket from Bess's bed.

"Go away," Bess muttered.

"No, I will not!" The owl emitted a shrill, ear-piercing shriek.

Bess sat up, startled. She had never heard Ulli's shriek before. It reverberated through the entire tree.

"You think you're the first creature to be thrown over, cast aside, jilted? No indeed."

Bess blinked. "What are you talking about?"

"You and your friend Will."

"So you've been spying on me?"

"No, not really."

"You have been. There's no 'not really' about it. But you missed one important point."

"What's that?"

"I did the jilting." She inhaled deeply. "Gone in a flash. He couldn't find me or follow me if he tried." Bess said this almost triumphantly.

"Oh." Ulli paused. "So you've mastered invisibility? How cunning," Ulli replied nastily. "So it worked."

"What?"

"The wand and the invisibility spell. Finally."

"Yes." Then Bess burst into sobs again.

"Well, make yourself visible and go back and say you're sorry that you acted so rashly."

"But I had no choice."

"No choice?"

Bess drew her face close to the owl's. "Ulli, I have to tell you something terrible."

And so Bess told the story of the hummingbird Stellina.

Ulli sighed. "So for all these years Stellina's soul has been trapped in glass, and now you broke the glass, released the soul, and Stellina flew off."

"Yes, that is the good part of the story."

"But the bad part is not Will Darlington's fault. It's your parents'. Will did not know their devilish methods."

"I know that, but still. He bought the figurine."

"And you released it. Would he have bought it if he'd known?"

"I don't know." Bess shrugged and began to cry again.

"Well, let me tell you another story that could end just as tragically."

It took a long time for Ulli to tell her what he suspected the Wickhams' intentions were for Estrella.

When Ulli finished, Bess gasped. "A new oven? Large enough for a girl? They plan to cast her in glass. And they call me a witch?"

"Bess, dear, this is a call for action. If there was a time to act, it is now!"

It was several minutes before Bess spoke again. "So you think they want to make one of these vanities by using Estrella? Steal her soul? Just like they have done with the animals in their awful oven fires?" Ulli nodded.

"Ulli, do you know the spirit wood?"

"Yes, it's not far from the glass house."

"Exactly. Spirit wood is dreaded by glassmakers. It does

not burn well. It slows the heat, delays the rise of the temperatures in the ovens. It almost infects the ovens like some sort of scourge. It spoils the cristallos so they cannot melt properly. But . . ."

"But what?" Ulli asked.

"It takes a lot of spirit wood to spoil the cristallos. To get all that wood into the glass house and into the fires without being noticed would be difficult."

"Nonsense, my girl. Your wand! Your invisibility talents! If anyone can do it, you can!"

31

COLD FIRES

Even in her invisible state, Bess found it frightening to be back in the glass house. She had just returned with her latest load of spirit wood, which had made the fires stubbornly cool. Hearing footsteps coming down the stairs to the hot shop, she quickly scurried into the back room, where all the most recent work was on shelves waiting to be shipped. A terrible feeling overcame her. She might be invisible to the rest of the world, but the crystal animals saw right through this mantle of invisibility. They growled. They bared their teeth. Bunnies turned monstrous. Hummingbirds grotesque with fury. A glass snail seemed to evacuate its shell and turn into a fanged snake. Her invisibility felt as frayed as an old threadbare shawl. She heard the voices of Lavinia and Charles.

"What is it with these fires?" Charles moaned.

"Charles, I'm not going to think about it now. This evening is the ball. I have to devote all my attention to getting our daughters ready."

"Yes," said Olivia.

"Mamma, my hair is not behaving. I need to add sausage curls. You know, the kind that you pin close together. We bought some pins in the village. Where are they?" Rose whined.

"But we didn't buy enough for both of us. And they'll go better with my French frizz style," Olivia snapped.

"Girls, I don't want you arguing. We have drawers full of hairpieces. Certainly, there are enough for the two of you.

"I want my hair done in that new, fashionable egg shape with high coils. Very high, like Princess Myrtle."

"Stop arguing about hairdos and Princess Myrtle!" their father boomed.

"Yes, hush, girls. Father is upset because the fires have mysteriously cooled." Their mother had dropped her voice.

"Oh!" both daughters said abruptly.

Then Rose, who often tried to be the peacemaker, spoke. "Well, as Mamma often says, there's always another day. And perhaps, since Papa has rented a coach and driver for us, today would not be a perfect day for our . . . our . . .

experiment." Rose paused for a moment. "It might smell different, you know?"

Olivia giggled. "Roasted lamb for the shepherdess!"

I'm definitely invisible, Bess thought, as a wave of nausea overtook her, *but I might throw up.* Then an idea came to her. *I must get Estrella out of this house and to the ball. I must create a dress for her. If I could do this and somehow send her off to the ball, and if a young man, any young man, would fall in love with her, then she would be safe . . .*

It seemed to take forever for the sisters to dress for the ball, but when at last they went off in the coach, there was just one problem—Arwan the dog. Even though she was invisible, if Bess came close to the cellar, Arwan would begin to growl and nip at the air. It was as if an invisible wall of glass had descended between Bess and Estrella. None of her spells to rid herself of the dog seemed to work. Indeed, the harder she tried, the more vicious the dog became. Bess was not sure what was happening. Why was the dog sensing her presence? She thought she had mastered invisibility.

Not quite!

The voice was familiar. "Grannie?"

We are masters of none. Not invisibility. Not even the stars.

"But what am I to do, Grannie?"

A luminous sphere had begun to float down and hover over Arwan. The dog began to tremble. Its knees buckled, and then it collapsed on the ground into a deep sleep. *Now get to work*, a voice, her grannie's voice, whispered very close to her ear. Then the bright sphere began to dissolve.

Bess entered the cellar, and in an instant, the words, the charms, came to her. She began to wave the wand in delicate gestures, as if tracing an invisible picture in the air.

First there was the dress: a cumulus of sparkling white, as if a galaxy had wrapped Estrella in a gown made in the heavens, yet trimmed with the blossoms of tiniest violets—not glass or crystal, but real violets. And it was then that Estrella gasped. "I can see you at last. You are Bess!"

"Indeed I am. Now listen carefully: you will go to the ball, but when the clock begins to strike midnight, the violets on your dress will begin to wilt and you must leave."

"Yes, yes, of course." Estrella looked down at her feet. "But I have no shoes."

"Oh dear, I forgot." Bess crouched down and tapped each foot with the wand. Estrella's feet suddenly seemed luminous.

"Glass slippers!"

"Why not?" Bess said. "It will be a magical night for you." But even Bess did not know how magical that night would become.

With another wave of her wand, a pumpkin with wheels appeared and rolled up to the cellar window.

"My pumpkin!" Estrella gasped.

One more wave of the wand and Arwan was transformed into a horse.

"Now off you go!"

"Off I go," Estrella whispered to herself as she gathered her gown and stepped daintily into the coach.

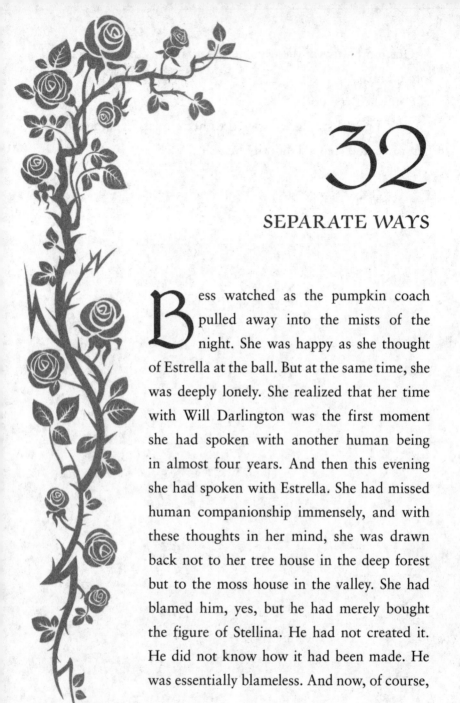

32

SEPARATE WAYS

Bess watched as the pumpkin coach pulled away into the mists of the night. She was happy as she thought of Estrella at the ball. But at the same time, she was deeply lonely. She realized that her time with Will Darlington was the first moment she had spoken with another human being in almost four years. And then this evening she had spoken with Estrella. She had missed human companionship immensely, and with these thoughts in her mind, she was drawn back not to her tree house in the deep forest but to the moss house in the valley. She had blamed him, yes, but he had merely bought the figure of Stellina. He had not created it. He did not know how it had been made. He was essentially blameless. And now, of course,

Stellina was free. Just as she had this thought, a shooting star passed over her head. But no! It was not a shooting star but . . . but . . . Stellina. How could that be? Hummingbirds rarely flew at night.

"Stellina! What are you doing here?"

"The night is growing darker. I'll guide you to the moss house."

"But why?" Bess asked. "You are free now."

"But you aren't."

She looked at the bird fluttering radiantly like a jewel in the night. She could think of nothing to say. So she walked on in the glittering wake of Stellina.

She sensed there was something different about the moss house the moment she stepped into it. It had not been that long since she had fled the house, but it seemed now that it could have been a hundred years ago. Cobwebs hung from the rafters. Dust was thick on the shelves, and many of the books were gone—but where? Even the garden, she now realized, was a tangle of weeds. How much time had passed since she had last been here? She walked into the study and gasped when she saw the scattered shards of the glass figurine from which Stellina's soul, trapped for so long, had burst. She looked about. This house, too, this moss cottage, had once held another soul, and now that soul was gone— gone. Bess collapsed on the floor, sobbing. "What have I done? What have I done!"

She walked through the back door of the cottage and

glanced across another valley.

"What are those lights in the distance?" she asked Stellina.

"Wynmore, the royal palace," Stellina answered.

"That's where the ball is tonight."

"What ball?" Stellina asked.

"The prince's ball. My sisters are attending."

"May their souls be broken!" Stellina muttered in a voice that Bess had never before heard.

Bess began to walk down into the valley.

"Where are you going?" Stellina asked.

"To the ball . . ." Bess answered softly.

Throngs had gathered in the town of Wynmore to celebrate the return of the prince. There was music and jugglers and even a dancing bear. It was as if two celebrations were occurring side by side—one inside the palace for the gentry of the county and one for the ordinary people. There was even food, all free, that the prince had provided for the townspeople. No one seemed to notice Bess as she wandered through the throngs, enjoying the burble of conversation and the noises of merrymaking that surrounded her.

She wasn't sure how long she had been in the town when she felt as if someone was pushing her toward the edges of the gathering. She planted her feet firmly. There was a harsh whisper in her ear. "No, you don't!"

"I beg your pardon, sir!"

Bess wheeled about to find a bewhiskered man with a sliver of a mouth that now curled up into a sneering smile. "I got her!" he called out. A net dropped over her, and she soon found herself being trussed up like a chicken.

"A witch for roasting!" someone shouted out.

Inside the palace was the sparkling world of the gentry. Ladies steeped in ruffles and silk swirled across the floor with gentlemen in finely tailored waistcoats. Estrella sat in a chair at the edge of the ballroom. Luckily neither Rose nor Olivia recognized her. They had all danced with the prince. To Estrella, the prince seemed like the most boring person in the world. Distracted and encased in a stony silence, he had a most unroyal awkwardness about him and did little to hide his boredom. It looked as if he was coming across the ballroom to dance with her next. *Oh dear!* she thought. *Whatever shall we talk about?* Just as he was making his slight bow in front of her, a courtier came up to him.

"Your Highness, Dottore Piero D'Angelo has arrived to fix the Galileo."

"Galileo!" Estrella gulped. "You own a Galileo telescope?"

"Yes, you know what one is?"

"Of course I do."

The prince tipped his head and regarded her. She was pretty, but definitely a country girl. Where would she have learned such things?

"I . . . I love the stars," she said simply.

"Well, come along, then. Perhaps you'd like a closer look. A ballroom is not the place to look for stars."

"Certainly not," Estrella whispered.

Minutes later, as she stepped out onto the highest roof of the palace, she thought to herself, *I am back, freed from Earth. Perhaps a stranger on my own planet, but now I am free to wander the sky again.*

"Piero, so good of you to come," the prince said.

A tall man had his back to both Estrella and the prince as he pressed his eye to the telescope. "I came a few weeks back, but they said you were at your lodge in the valley. Now I've returned with better tools for correcting the scope's alignment."

Estrella watched him as he made slight adjustments to the telescope. His body moved with a particular grace.

"Yes, yes, I was in the valley."

"But we are both here now." He spun around, away from the eyepiece of the telescope to face the prince. "Prince William, always an honor."

"Oh, please just call me Will," the prince said.

But Piero's jaw dropped as his gaze fell upon Estrella. *I believe I am seeing another star before me. An* estrella del terra!

And then Estrella herself tipped her head slightly to take in the gentleness of his eyes. Yes, he was handsome, but it came from an empathy deep within him. It seemed he could not take his eyes away from her while the prince fiddled with some knobs on the Galileo telescope. Nor could she take her eyes from him. It was as if they were beyond words, entering a new universe where there was only light and stars.

"Here, come take a look, Piero."

"Yes, Your Highness." Tearing his eyes away from Estrella, he walked the few steps over to the scope and pressed his eye to the lens.

"And the problem?" the prince asked, after a minute or so.

"A misalignment of the lens, I believe," Piero D'Angelo murmured as the clock began to chime midnight. At that same moment, a violet wilted on Estrella's gown and dropped from the bodice. "The telescope is too close to the bell tower. The vibrations cause the misalignment," he said, turning around.

"In other words, they must stop the clock?" asked the prince.

But the world seemed to have already stopped for Estrella as her eyes and those of Piero D'Angelo locked. She could not move. Violet blossoms were collecting at her feet. There was a gulf of silence between them as the chimes tolled. *What next?* Estrella wondered. But there was no next. She tore across the terrace. The din of the tolling bells in her ears was maddening. Her dress was turning to rags as she ran, and one slipper slid from her foot. It did not break but was caught in a cross fire of moonbeams. The lens keeper of Greenwich bent down to retrieve it. He stared at the glass slipper, which seemed in his eyes to contain a universe, but it was a universe that was receding from him. One shoe he held in his hand, but the sound of the other on the foot of the lovely Estrella was growing dimmer and dimmer.

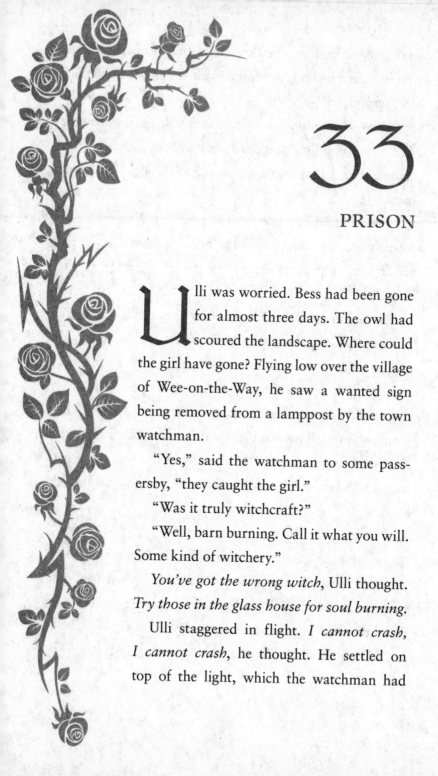

33

PRISON

Ulli was worried. Bess had been gone for almost three days. The owl had scoured the landscape. Where could the girl have gone? Flying low over the village of Wee-on-the-Way, he saw a wanted sign being removed from a lamppost by the town watchman.

"Yes," said the watchman to some passersby, "they caught the girl."

"Was it truly witchcraft?"

"Well, barn burning. Call it what you will. Some kind of witchery."

You've got the wrong witch, Ulli thought. *Try those in the glass house for soul burning.*

Ulli staggered in flight. *I cannot crash, I cannot crash,* he thought. He settled on top of the light, which the watchman had extinguished minutes before. He wilfed, growing thinner and thinner. His body appeared to almost flow into the slender lamppost.

Prison. Bess in prison . . . But she could get out, couldn't she? The invisibility charm . . . but what if she didn't have her wand . . . Ulli continued listening to the night watchman speak.

"They netted her over in the town of Wynmore. The whole town was celebrating the prince's return to the palace in the royal plaza. There was to be a grand ball that night."

"Netted her, did they? Is that how they catch witches?"

The night watchman chuckled. "Guess so. Never caught one myself."

Ulli had to steady himself on top of the post. But surely Bess could escape. She had mastered the invisibility charm with her wand. But what if she didn't have her wand? What if she had dropped it in Wynmore when she was being netted? It was as if a swarm of bees was buzzing through Ulli's head.

At the same time, Bess, now in a cell in the Wynmore prison, heard the roar of a crowd outside the barred window. The voices were cheering. Were they celebrating her capture? She heard the jailer coming down the hallway.

"What's the noise outside?"

"Not for you, witchy. For the prince. They are celebrating his return."

"Return? From where?"

"Prince William has a habit of disappearing on occasion. Some call him the Hermit Prince. A studious fellow. Cares not for grand balls. But there was a big one for him two nights ago."

"Yes, so I heard," muttered Bess. Her hand went in her deep pocket for her wand. It was perhaps the fiftieth time she'd reached for her wand. But it was gone. She had lost it when she had been netted. She had never felt such utter despair in her life.

"So a few nights ago was the ball, and today there is a parade in his honor. The parade goes right by the jail. You'll see him on his charger in his full Regimental Commanders uniform, red and bright with medals and the royal badges and the golden collar, of course. Quite a handsome fellow."

There was a sudden blare of trumpets. "He's coming! He's coming!" The guard's voice rose with excitement. "Now don't you go casting any spells, witch!"

Bess remained silent and pressed her face against the bars.

First came an honor guard, the grenadiers who rode in front of the prince. Then came a slender young man in a red uniform, spangled with medals and, yes, a golden collar. The music and the cheers blended together in a deafening roar. The prince's horse reared slightly, and his hat fell off. He seemed delighted by the mishap and smiled broadly as the crowd cheered even louder. Bess opened her eyes wide.

"Will!" The word was like an inhalation of breath more than an actual name. "WILL!" she screamed at the top of her lungs. "WILL DARLINGTON!"

Meanwhile, in the plaza beneath the palace, Ulli skimmed back and forth in flight. The owl did several low-flying passes as servants from the palace cleaned up from the revelers two nights before. A young palace servant looked up. "Edna," she said to the girl working next to her. "What is that owl doing flying about? It's been back and forth a dozen times or more. It's a barn owl, I believe."

"Ghost owls, they call them where I come from, Abby."

Abby bent over again to pick up something odd. Not a half-eaten sausage or sweets on a stick or a half-eaten fried fish, but something decidedly inedible.

"What do you suppose this is?" Abby asked. "At first I thought it was a sugar crystal stick." And just as she said the word *stick*, Ulli plunged down and snatched the wand from the girl's hand. The girl fell down. "What in the world?" She gasped. "I've been attacked!"

Scant minutes later, another girl on the other side of the city gasped the very same words—"What in the world!"—just as Ulli flew past the barred cell windows and slid the wand through.

The jailer heard her squeal of delight and came rushing. He stood dumbfounded as he watched Bess Wickham, the witch of Wee-on-the-Way, dissolve before his eyes.

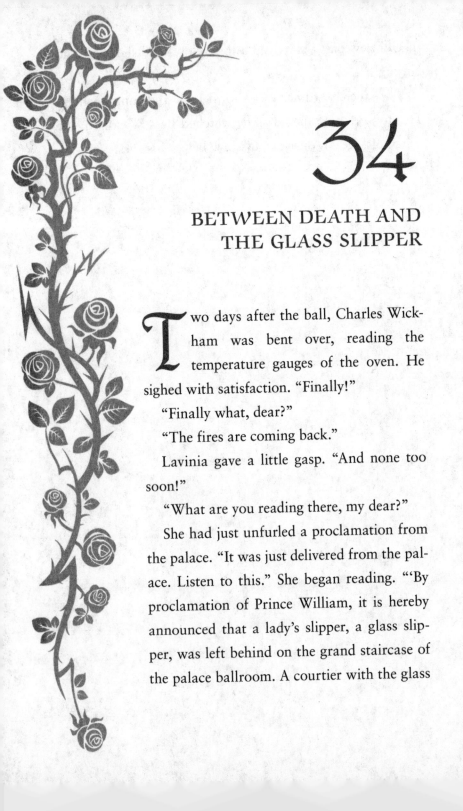

34

BETWEEN DEATH AND
THE GLASS SLIPPER

Two days after the ball, Charles Wickham was bent over, reading the temperature gauges of the oven. He sighed with satisfaction. "Finally!"

"Finally what, dear?"

"The fires are coming back."

Lavinia gave a little gasp. "And none too soon!"

"What are you reading there, my dear?"

She had just unfurled a proclamation from the palace. "It was just delivered from the palace. Listen to this." She began reading. "'By proclamation of Prince William, it is hereby announced that a lady's slipper, a glass slipper, was left behind on the grand staircase of the palace ballroom. A courtier with the glass slipper will call upon all families who attended the ball to find the foot for which it was made.'"

The two girls turned to their father. "Papa, did you make such a glass slipper?" Olivia asked.

"No. Don't you recall that we went to the cobbler and had a pretty satin pair made for each of you to match your dresses? Pretty and very expensive, I might add."

"Well, what does that matter?" Lavinia said. "If it fits, it fits. And it could fit either one of you."

At that moment they realized that Ella was standing in the doorway. They froze as they saw her holding a glass slipper. "Perhaps it's this one?" She held the elegant slipper aloft.

"Seize her, Charles!" Lavinia screeched as she ran to open the gathering oven's door. Estrella dropped the shoe she had been holding. They all were stunned as it shattered on the floor. A great wind of hot air blasted from the oven. Estrella staggered. She felt her dress ripping as Charles seized the skirt. Then Olivia grabbed her hair. The two together were wrestling her to the ground. Estrella had only one thought in her head. *I shall not die. I shall not die. I shall kill before I die.* She sunk her teeth into Olivia's ankle. Charles was cursing her and reached down now to grab her neck, but she raised her knee and kicked him in the groin. He doubled over. Flames were leaping from the oven door, threatening to devour them. At the same moment, Bess stepped out from behind the oven. She lifted her wand. Sparks flew from it. Estrella gasped as she watched Rose, Olivia, and their parents suddenly grow rigid, and then within seconds turn transparent. Their eyes glared in a glassy, paralytic horror. There were tiny crackling sounds as hair-thin fractures spread through their bodies. The noise grew louder and was followed by the din of shattering glass as the Wickham family, one by one, crashed to the floor.

Estrella looked down at her feet, stunned at the shards of broken glass in which she was standing.

"I am whole," she whispered. "Whole."

"This way," Bess said, beckoning to her. "Walk carefully. Don't cut yourself."

As soon as they were outside and standing in the vegetable garden, Estrella turned to Bess, who had Ulli perched on her shoulder.

"Bess, how did you get here?"

Bess's mouth drew into an odd little smile. "Hard to explain." And she waved her wand. Then there was a splintering sound as the glass house began to crack, then shatter. A sudden wind swept around them, and the shattered fragments swirled up like a dazzling tornado into opalescent clouds.

From across a field, two figures appeared on the horizon.

Estrella gasped, "I do believe that is the prince and Piero."

"Not a prince," Bess said softly. "It's Will, Will Darlington from the valley beyond."

"No, no, not at all," Estrella protested. "I've met him.

Not from any valley . . . from here . . . the palace. That is the prince. I danced with him."

"I've met him, too," Bess said. "But who is Piero? Another prince?"

"Oh, definitely not," Estrella replied in a trembling voice. "Piero is an astronomer."

"What?" Bess said. "I'm confused."

"I'm not," the prince said. "Nor is Piero."

Something soft thumped behind them.

"What's that?" Bess said, and then opened her eyes wide. "A bunny!" she gasped. At the same time, a robin alighted on her shoulder, making a *tuk* sound. Soon hummingbirds were swooping through the night. There was the *baa* of a baby lamb and the harsh caw of a blue jay. A small red fox scampered by. The night stirred with souls long trapped in glass, which were now set free. A puppy ran around Bess's legs, yapping and jumping. She immediately recognized it as the neighbor's dog that had been lost shortly after her grandmother had died.

"They've come back! All of them!" Ulli hooted softly.

"Not all of them," Bess whispered. And then, just as a full moon began to rise, a green light seemed to suffuse the night. An immense silver wolf stepped forward.

"Lear!" Bess tore across the rubble of the shattered house and fell to her knees, flinging her arms around the neck of the wolf. Then leaping out of the darkness came Jenig and her pups, which were no longer pups, but with their own pups tagging behind.

Years lost were suddenly regained. Time had recovered and mended this brand-new, beautifully shattered world.

"But how can this be?" Estrella wondered aloud.

"Anything is possible," Piero replied.

Will Darlington now stepped forward and took Bess's hand and, looking into her eyes, said, "Yes, anything is possible. A prince can become Will Darlington again and love a girl named Bess and study birds."

"But, Will, do I have to be a princess? Can I still love you without being a princess? Without wearing a crown?"

"Of course you can. You can become the royal guardian of all creatures."

"Not *royal*, please. Just Bess the guardian."

"And," Piero began to speak, "a lens keeper can take his true love back to Greenwich and live in complete happiness with her, tending the lenses of the great refracting telescope."

Tending the lenses. The words were like music in Estrella's ears.

"This must be the happily ever after," Bess whispered to herself as she squeezed Will Darlington's hand. Estrella looked up in that single moment at dusk, when both the sun and the moon shared the sky. She blinked in disbelief when that rarest of astronomical events came true, as Venus touched the disc of the setting sun and a barn owl flew into the coming night, its shadow printed against the rising moon.

Epilogue

THE PRINCE AND THE WITCH

Centuries later, where the moss cottage once stood, there was a sign welcoming visitors, and all bird watchers especially.

Welcome, friends, to the Crop Shire Bird and Nature Sanctuary. The foundation of the cottage that you see before you was once the home of a prince and a witch who fell in love with each other and ran away together to live in this cottage more than two hundred years ago. They loved all creatures and vowed to protect them as best they could. For some reason, and we don't know why, there is a tradition here that no glass is permitted on the grounds, with the exception of the glass of binoculars for viewing animals or that of telescopes for the stars. Please abide by this single rule and put all glass bottles in the refuse bins provided at the entrance.